UNHALLOWED

BLACK OPS PARANORMAL POLICE DEPARTMENT:
SINISTER VENGEANCE BOOK ONE

JOHN P. LOGSDON

CHRISTOPHER P. YOUNG

CRIMSON MYTH
PRESS

Published by: Crimson Myth Press (www.CrimsonMyth.com)

Cover art: Audrey Logsdon (www.AudreyLogsdon.com)

Thanks to TEAM ASS!
Advanced Story Squad

This is the first line of readers of the series. Their job is to help me keep things in check and also to make sure I'm not doing anything way off base in the various story locations!

(listed in alphabetical order by first name)

Anne Morando
Audrey Cienki
Bennah Phelps
Carolyn Fielding
Dana Arms Audette
Debbie Tily
Hal Bass
Jan Gray
Jim Stoltz
John Debnam
Julie Peckett
Karen Hollyhead
Kathleen Portig
Kevin Frost
Larry Diaz Tushman
LeAnne Benson
Mary Letton
Megan McBrien
Mike Slaan Helas
Nat Fallon

Penny Noble
Rob Hill
Sandee Lloyd
Sara Mason Branson
Scott Reid
Sharon Harradine
Terri Adkisson

Thanks to Team DAMN
Demented And Magnificently Naughty

This crew is the second line of readers who get the final draft of the story, report any issues they find, and do their best to inflate my fragile ego.

(listed in alphabetical order by first name)

Adam Goldstein, Amy Robertson, Beth Adams, Bobbi Mooney, Brett Wickersham, Carrie Markgraf Blum, Celeste Canning, Cindy Deporter, Doug Carlson, Emma Porter, George Coughlin III, Heather Noon, Heidi Gaspie, Helen Day, Ian R. Jackson, Ingrid Schijven, Jacky Oxley, Janine Corcoran, Jen Cooper, Juli Nash, Leslie Watts, Lindsay McDonald, Lisa Camden Cripe, Lynette Wood, Malcolm Robertson, MaryAnn Sims, Melissa Parsons, Patty Keck, Scott Ackermann, Scott Oszvart, Scottie Hinton, Stacey Stein, Stephanie Wurtz, Tim Hubbard, Tony Dawson, Travis Sleeper, Victoria Mckenna.

CHAPTER 1

It's better to delay mourning than to become another who is mourned.

— GARRICK - HOUSE OF SINISTER

*S*creams echoed through my head as I watched members of House Sinister being slaughtered via the Rite of Decimation.

There were three Houses working together to destroy mine. Varaz, Mathen, and Tross. Minor players who were obviously looking for their seat at the big table.

From my perch on the fourth floor, overlooking the alcove, the battles played out like a macabre scene from a horror film. Blades slashed and parried with such speed that only advanced eyes could track their flowing grace. Blood spilled on all sides as the murderous bastards poured in, pressing inevitably toward the Head Elder.

His death would signal that Sinister had fallen.

But that wouldn't end the House.

For that to happen, every last member would have to be dispatched.

That was hellion law.

As if connected by some cosmic force, Garrick, the head of the Guard, looked up, his eyes meeting mine. My teacher since I was a child, he'd always treated me with dignity and respect. Plus, he was a rowdy and foul-mouthed bastard who taught me to drink, swear, and fight dirty.

Garrick was the best warrior the House had ever seen.

I was nothing but a peon as far as the elders were concerned, but Garrick had seen ability in me, and it was his wish that I would one day rise up the ranks and replace him as the head of the Guard.

The one thing he'd instilled in me over everything else, though, was that the House came first.

Period.

That sentiment was repeated in his eyes as he stared up at me.

Unfortunately, one of the assassins nearest him had followed the gaze and spotted me as well. He pointed, causing a sea of heads to spin and take a mental snapshot of yet another victim to notch their blades.

Garrick redoubled his efforts, cutting and stabbing like a man possessed.

"The House must survive," he yelled at me as I felt the magic welling up in my hands. "Remember your oath! Remember your duty!"

If *any* member of the House remained alive, the House remained alive. No strings could be left uncut. If there were any stragglers, the Rite of Decimation would be considered a failure.

"Run! Now!"

Garrick fell seconds later as multiple blades entered his flesh, taking a part of me with him.

As his body sank to the ground, so did my stomach.

I'd been punched, kicked, thrown, cut, and even shot over my years training with the Guard, but never had I felt such devastation as I'd suffered in that moment.

My mentor was dead.

"Stop where you are," called out a hellion who stepped off the stairs at the top of the landing.

I turned to face him, feeling a mix of rage and fear. I wasn't afraid of dying, but I *was* afraid of failing to deliver on Garrick's dying command. He'd spent years putting his faith in me, giving me a chance to become more than just a concubine, like my mother before me.

He deserved my best and I was damn sure going to give it all I had.

But fighting the pain was proving tougher than I'd expected.

One day I knew I'd be the one to replace him as the head of the Guard. He'd told me that on more than one occasion.

Sadly, that day had arrived.

He'd counted on me through thick and thin, he'd commanded me in the moment of his death, and my oath to put the House before my own desire told me that now was not the time to mourn him.

So, I shoved down the pain and focused on survival.

The assassin stood with sword drawn. He had four

goons with him as well. They were from the House of Varaz, which was clear from the red V on each jacket.

"Are you guys in a boy band or something?" I asked, noting how they even had their hair slicked back the same way.

"Don't move," warned the leader, clearly ignoring my jab as his comrades glanced back and forth at one another. "And don't try any tricks either."

"Or what?" I replied, lacing my voice with sarcasm while seeking a way to escape. "You'll kill me?"

"That's an inevitability," he answered, taking a cautious step in my direction as his goons began to spread out. "It'll be quick. I promise."

"I'm sure your wife hears that every night," I shot back, spotting my exit.

The lackeys giggled, but quickly hushed as their leader's enraged eyes peered at them.

I'd clearly touched a nerve.

Good.

Fortunately, I was young. By hellion standards, anyway. The assassins saw me as nothing but a gnat who needed squashing. If they had seen me as something threatening, they would have sent more assassins.

"Kill the little bitch," he commanded.

I'd already had both of my blades out, but taking down a group of assassin-level fighters wasn't exactly an easy thing to do, nor was it the smart thing. I *could* have unleashed a wave of fire at them that they would never have expected, but that would only attract more of their kind. Using magic and having the ability to dual-wield swords was great, but it wasn't enough to take down an army. My only hope of keeping my word to Garrick was to get the hell out of there.

Garrick's words came back to me, and they were right.

I needed an escape.

The Guard's quarters were the only option.

Thankfully, it was behind me.

I spun and ran for it, sliding my blades back into their sheaths before bolting through the door and slamming it shut, twisting the key an instant before the handle turned.

"Open the door and we'll kill you mercifully!"

"Go fuck yourself," I yelled back as I crossed the creaking floor.

It was the only room that had a window near the vines that draped the walls. Instead of falling from four stories up, I could climb down.

I was halfway to the ground when I heard the door crash in above.

That caused me to drop the remaining distance, rolling upon landing.

"Now what?" I hissed aloud, looking around as the Varaz boys started climbing down the vines.

If only Garrick was here.

Pain threatened to sink in again.

No!

There was no time for that now.

The problem was that there was no escaping them in the Badlands. At least not through the tunnels or caves. Getting to the Strip wasn't going to happen. It was way too far. Hell wasn't an option either for the same reason. Netherworld Proper *was* an option, but I'd probably get returned within a few months in order to avoid there being an international incident.

That left the Forbidden Loch.

It was the one place that hellions avoided like blessed water.

This had to do with the fact that it was considered holy ground.

Now, I know what you're thinking: How can there be 'holy ground' in the Badlands? You should also be wondering how hellions like me, who were essentially demons mixed with dragon blood, would give a shit about anything holy anyway.

My response?

You've read one too many books on the subject of religion, and you don't realize that it was all made up by us.

Regardless, the reason it was considered holy ground to us was that there was some mysterious shit that happened there. If anything, based on the stories I'd been told, it should be considered *unholy* ground.

Too bad it was my only option at this point.

I bolted right toward the Forbidden Loch and dove in without even dipping my toe in the water to check the temperature.

It was cold.

Ice cold.

It was also pitch black.

But I didn't need eyes to know where I was going. The books and drawings made it clear exactly where the portal entrance was housed.

All the way at the bottom of the loch.

The water shifted and I heard the sound of waves splashing above me, signaling that my pursuers were more afraid of failure than they were of defiling holy ground. That, or they knew something about this place that I didn't.

My lungs began to burn and my ears popped as the pressure built up around me, but I pushed forward. If I was going to die, it wouldn't be due to giving up on account of discomfort.

No, the bastards on my tail were going to have to kill me.

Straight out.

And I had no intentions of making their quest easy, either.

CHAPTER 2

*J*ust as I was feeling my brain starting to fold under the strain of the dive, I saw a faint light and swam harder.

The water was beginning to warm and the pressure was noticeably lessening. A few more pushes and I broke through a barrier of some sort, crashing to the ground and drying instantly.

It took a few seconds of heaving to get my breathing back under control.

I stood and looked up, seeing a mass of water hovering above, pulsing and rippling as though someone had thrown a rock into an upside-down still lake.

There were five bodies slowly coming into view as well, though.

"Shit," I hissed as I frantically scanned the area.

The portal was against the wall on the other side of the room.

I double-timed my run and stopped in front of it just

as the thuds of predatory bodies crashed through the ceiling of water behind me.

"There she is," the leader yelled, choking and sputtering. "Kill her!"

I glanced back, seeing them getting to their feet.

"Wait," I said, putting my hand up. Surprisingly, they did. "I have an offer for you."

The main guy motioned to calm his goons. There was no way he would actually agree to anything I may have offered, but I was just looking to buy time. I had no idea how the portal worked, after all.

"You know I can't accept any deals during a Rite of Decimation," he said with a tilt of his head. "Therefore," he continued, sniffing the air, "this must be some type of ruse."

"Damn," I replied, doing my best to look defeated. "Obviously, I can't match wits with someone of your intellect." I sighed. "You're right. I *was* trying to fool you." I gave him a grin that was befitting my House's name. "It's just that making a full-grown flame beast appear takes a lot of effort, and it also takes about a minute for it to appear, so I needed a little time."

"A what?" asked one of the lackeys.

With a dramatic lift of my finger, I pointed to a dark area of the room. There was nothing there, of course, but they didn't know that.

I cackled for added effect.

"What did you do?" asked the leader, swallowing hard. "Nobody told us you were adept with advanced magic."

I was actually well-beyond what the average hellion was capable of doing with magic. We could all summon the dark mark and do some basic flames and energy, but with my ability to dual-wield also came a higher capability with magic. I could cast fireballs and ice storms, and was pretty adept with shields and healing, but it wore me out something fierce. With people chasing me, one poorly placed spell would only serve to drain my strength. Regardless, summoning a flame beast, or *any* beast, wasn't going to happen. I wasn't *that* good.

But I also wasn't dumb enough to tell him that.

"Nobody told me that you were an asshole, either," I said, keeping him on his toes, "but here we are."

"You incorrigible little—"

"Ah-ah-ah," I interrupted him, wagging my finger in warning. "You *do* know what happens if you kill someone who has created a flame beast, right?"

His eyes darted back and forth.

"No," he said at length.

Neither did I, especially since there was no such thing as a flame beast.

"Well," I said, turning my back to him, "I suppose you'll find out soon enough."

I heard footsteps.

"Wait!" the leader commanded. "Tell us what will happen or we'll…uh…"

"Kill me, right?" I said while giving him a look over my shoulder. "You've already used that one. How sad that they sent you idiots. It honestly damages my ego a bit, if I'm being honest."

I'd found the switch and flicked it, carefully hiding the panel's lights from their eyes.

There was a loud growl.

"What the fuck was that?" I said, jolting upright and spinning around. They all had their swords out and were forming into a circle. "You guys heard that, too, right?"

"Wouldn't that be your flame beast?" asked the leader, his eyes burning like embers.

"Oh, yeah," I said. "Uh…that's right."

"There's no damn flame beast," he shot back. "She's using tricks to make those sounds. Kill her and let's get out of here."

Closing my eyes, I jumped into the portal.

Everything went completely still and quiet, including my mind.

Maybe that meant one of those pricks had gotten me before I made it through? I hadn't felt a blade or an arrow or a knife, but maybe it had been the perfect kill shot?

I carefully opened one eye and found that I was being engulfed in a fountain of light. It wasn't a bright white light, but rather a luminescence so dark that it glowed black.

There was a peace to being in here, but I didn't know why.

I gently spun, feeling like a feather on the wind, until I spotted the five hellions who were bent on my destruction. Their faces held looks of rage, telling me that they had *not* killed me. So, whatever I was currently experiencing had to do with the portal.

There was another presence in the room with them as well. I doubted it was a flame beast—that would have been funny—but it certainly wasn't friendly.

Child, said a voice that shook me to the core, *you have entered the Forbidden Loch.*

I replied with a thought.

Yes.

Why?

I was looking around, seeking the voice, but I couldn't spot anything.

My House is going through a Rite of Decimation, and I am seeking escape.

I see, the voice said. *And your House is?*

Sinister.

Verifying.

The calming peace ceased for a terrifying instant as the world exploded in my head, showing my psyche visions of wars, violence, and hate. It was as though every horrible thing done by *any* of my ancestors and contemporaries was being sewn into my very being.

You are indeed of the House of Sinister.

Yeah, I know.

I'm sorry to inform you that you are the only remaining member of your House as well.

So the decimation had been completed. Well, except for me, obviously. That made my survival even more urgent.

I shouldn't have been surprised, though. It wasn't like these things were done without a ton of planning. Again, hellions did not tolerate failure kindly.

But they hadn't counted on me running.

They'd probably just assumed all the young ones would raise their blades and defiantly charge like we'd been trained to do.

I had never been one to shy away from fighting, but Garrick had done more than show me the uses of the

13

blade. He'd crafted my common sense as well. Even more importantly, he gave me autonomy of thought. But even he instilled the importance of the House in the land of the hellions.

Legacy was everything.

But Garrick was gone.

They were all gone.

Every last one of them.

You are very fortunate, young one.

Peaceful or not, I couldn't help but squint at that statement.

I sure as fuck don't feel fortunate.

You are, it insisted. *Were you not the last of your House, I would have been unable to assist you.*

I blinked. *Huh?*

Only an elder of a House can use the divine portal, the thing explained.

I'm not an elder.

You are all that remains from the House of Sinister, my dear. That makes you the eldest in your clan. Therefore, by hellion law, you are not only an elder, you are the *elder.*

Oh.

That was a bit much to process.

As a hellion, twenty-seven was insanely young. This portal had just declared me to be the youngest elder in history.

The history I knew, anyway.

What about them? I asked, slowly pointing at the assassins who were following me. *Are they elders?*

I'd already assumed the main guy was, but his helpers looked like peons to me.

14

Moloch of Varaz is, which means the other four may follow him.

Well, at least I had the name of the lead guy now.

Ah, stated the voice, *it seems that one of them has fallen to the flame beast, so that means only three will follow along with him.*

The what? I replied, looking out to see the Varaz boys battling in slow motion against a monster who was covered in fire. *Wait, there's actually such a thing?*

Of course. It guards the holy grounds under the loch.

So *that's* where I'd gotten that name. I just kind of threw it out there, thinking it sounded reasonable enough to be real. Obviously, I'd heard about it somewhere during my training while growing up.

Great.

Not really, it replied.

I frowned.

Depends on your perspective, I suppose. I got my mind back in the game. *Anyway, why aren't they in here with me now?*

Because you are under my protection until I release you.

That was nice, but it wasn't like I could stay in here forever. Eventually I'd have to leave, and when that happened, I'd be the shortest living elder in the history of my people.

Where can I go? I asked, hoping the portal could give me some guidance here. *Even if that thing kills them, I'm dead if I go back into the Badlands, and that means my House is dead.*

I would recommend that you go topside, child.

Where the normals are? My question was nearly a shriek.

Yes. There you may possess a body, which will render you invisible to those who seek to destroy you.

My breath caught at the suggestion.

But that's forbidden, I rasped.

Yes, it agreed, *but your choices are limited. Would you rather forbidden or suicidal?* It paused. *Plus, let's not forget you're standing in the Forbidden Loch right now, so it's not like you're opposed to straying when it suits you.*

True, I replied, pursing my lips. *Okay, so topside then?*

That would be my recommendation.

I nodded, glancing to the hate on the faces bent on ending my life as they continued fighting against the flame beast.

Will they follow me?

The voice sounded sad when it answered. *I can do nothing to prevent it, I'm afraid. However, I shall reveal nothing regarding that of which we have spoken. However, they may ask where you chose to go and follow you. I can't refuse to answer that.*

That sucks, I said. *Kind of works out for them, doesn't it?*

Seek a body, the voice replied, obviously ignoring my question. *Possess the body and stay in it for as long as possible. Tell no one who you are. One day, you may return to claim the House of Sinister, as long as you survive at least a year. On that day, you will see your foes vanquished and you will fall under the protection of the Hellion Code.*

Right. Nifty. I glanced back at the four remaining idiots, including Moloch. *Uh...can I wait in here long enough for that flame beast to kill the rest of them?*

I'm afraid your time is already coming to a close, it replied.

I let out a slow breath.

Okay, send me topside, then. Someplace decent, preferably.

You'll be going to Los Angeles.

I swallowed. *Is that good?*

I've seen worse.

All right. I hardened my resolve. *What do I have to do?*

Prepare yourself, child. This will not be pleasant.

CHAPTER 3

When your life is on the line, your head and your gut will vie for your attention. *Always* trust your gut.

— GARRICK - HOUSE OF SINISTER

*T*he transport hurt like fuck. My insides felt like jelly for a few seconds and there was enough vomit laying on the road in front of me to validate that pain resulted in projection. My only hope was that my pursuers would have a momentary bout of illness, too.

Regardless, I had to get the hell out of here.

I didn't know anything about Los Angeles, and I certainly didn't know shit about being topside.

What I *did* know was that I was standing in the middle of a dimly lit street.

The area seemed seedy.

That didn't bother me as I highly doubted there was anything or anyone within the area that could pose a serious threat.

Still, I had to move along.

I ran down to the end of the street and looked both ways. To the left was a lit up skyline that had a bunch of tall buildings. To the right it was darker and the buildings looked more rundown.

"There," I heard the voice of Moloch yelling, "get her!" That was followed by a couple of retches. At least they'd felt the stab of the transport as badly as I had. "Chase her, you fools!"

My head said that diving into the shadows would be the safer bet, but my gut thought it smarter to run toward the lights.

I followed my gut.

My legs churned as I sniffed the air and scanned every potential outlet. One of the main things I noticed was that there was no perceptible difference between the Badlands and topside...as far as gravity and such went anyway. The air quality here did seem a little dank, but no worse than the area situated between the hellion Houses and the dragon Houses. It was called the Strip and I hadn't been there in a while, but I recalled that it was the model used when they'd built Las Vegas topside.

Too bad I was in Los Angeles.

I pushed away my trepidation and refocused on keeping my ass alive.

It didn't matter if I was here, Netherworld Proper, the Strip, or the nine levels of Hell...the goal was the same.

House Sinister's survival rested with me.

I glanced over my shoulder to find them gaining on me. Either I was spending too much time mired in concern over my surroundings or they were a lot faster than me. It could have been a combination of both, but one thing was for sure: running in a straight line clearly wasn't doing me any favors.

At the end of the stone building, I cut right and heard the sound of battle.

Focusing my vision, I caught sight of two groups punching, kicking, and stabbing each other.

A gun fired off, sparking me to get there even faster.

Dead bodies gave me a place to hide.

There was a time when hellions would possess topsiders who were alive, but that was banned in the Old War treaties. To possess a normal was punishable by permanent death, meaning you were sent through the Void, not the Vortex.

But my life meant more to House Sinister than it did to me. If I had to risk the Void, so be it.

I dove into the guy closest to me.

He shrieked as his rival stabbed him in the stomach.

It hurt me, too, but it wasn't going to kill me.

What *would* kill me was if Moloch and his pals arrived and finished the job. So, I hid deep in the gangbanger's mind, letting him feel the depth of pain as his life slowly slipped away.

Too bad him dying was a problem for me.

If the guy kicked it right there, Moloch would shred the body to make sure I wasn't hiding out. At least, that's what I would have done. There was no point in leaving anything unturned, especially with this much on the line.

Just as I was doing my damndest to make sure my House lived on, Moloch and his goons were going to do everything in their power to make sure it didn't. Their failure would result in not only their deaths, but the deaths of their immediate families. They could no doubt live with the fact that their spouses and children would be executed, but they likely had no desire to have their names disgraced throughout eternity.

"Who the fuck are you?" a muscular guy who was holding a knife barked at Moloch.

Moloch answered as expected, by way of his sword.

The guy's head bounced on the ground an instant later, causing everyone else in the immediate area to stop fighting.

Another gang member fired at Moloch, striking him in the shoulder.

Moloch grunted, grabbing at the wound for a moment. Slowly, he brought his eyes up in a scowl at the guy who had shot him. Two blinks later, Moloch flicked his wrist, sending his blade to stick through the head of the gun-toting idiot.

Obviously, these people had never fought hellions before.

"Rip them all apart," Moloch demanded. "She's in here somewhere. Find her!"

Shit.

People started hightailing it out of the area, running in all directions. As one dude ran past the guy I was in, I jumped into him instead.

This was done just in time, as one of Moloch's goons shredded the man I'd left behind.

It only took a second before he was hot on the trail of the guy I was in, too.

I may not have been as fast a runner as Moloch and his

goons, but I was faster than the average normal by far. This guy was moving so slowly that it damn near felt like I was power-walking.

"Fuck," I yelled as I separated from the dude and summoned my blades, spinning just in time to slice them across my pursuer's back as he stabbed the gangbanger in the kidney.

My strike was strong enough to throw him to the ground, but he spun and brought his blade up, blocking my followup swipe.

Fighting from your back was not easy, and I definitely had the goon dead to rights.

I stared down at the bastard at my feet with hate in my eyes, ready to show him what happens when the perfect arc of a blade rips through the groin.

"There," barked Moloch, pointing at me. "Get her!"

The clanging of swords and my revealing myself was all Moloch needed to spot me and resume the chase.

Damn it.

"Asshole," I hissed as I used the guy's marbles as my kick off point for a run.

CHAPTER 4

I took every corner, knowing that they'd overtake me otherwise. Even as it stood, they were gaining ground.

It was time to shake shit up.

One of the many things that Garrick had instilled in his Guard was that fighting wasn't always handled on a single plane. In other words, sometimes you had to scale walls to get to higher ground. Good thing climbing had come easy to me.

I slipped around the edge of the next building and caught sight of a dumpster by the wall. A quick scan told me that I could hit the lowest ledge of the window if I took the leap in stride.

It'd have to be a hell of a jump, though.

Cranking my legs for all they were worth, I launched myself up, landed my foot perfectly on the lip of the dumpster, and then pushed again.

My adrenaline had obviously been riding higher than I'd thought because I completely cleared the ledge and smashed directly through the window above it. Thankfully, there hadn't been any metal bars. That would have been the end of Sinister House.

Still, crashing through a window was *not* pleasant.

I had cuts all over my hands, arms, face, and neck. Plus, the framing on that window wasn't exactly forgiving. If I hadn't had years of extensive training, specifically in how to squash pain, I would have just laid on the floor and waited for Moloch to find me and finish the job.

It still took me a few seconds to gain my composure, though.

Once I did, I looked up to find two young men staring at me with their mouths agape. The scrawny one wore glasses and had a serious case of acne. The other was chubby with messy facial hair that ran down his neck. They were both wearing black capes and were seated at a table that housed books and a board of some sort. A red light shone down on the table.

"Holy shit, dude," the chubby one said. "It worked!"

"Uh…"

"It worked, Billy."

"Yeah," Billy breathed. "I see that, Mitch, but now what do we do?"

I studied them both as they quickly stuck their heads into books, flipping pages like they were searching for gold.

"Here, here, here," Mitch announced, stabbing his finger at one of the pages. "We're supposed to demand that she…" He paused, gulping. "That she lay with us."

Billy's eyes grew wide as they both stared at each other in shock.

"Lay with you?" I said in a dark voice.

Mitch gulped.

"You sure that's what it says, man?" asked Billy, looking as terrified as he should have looked.

That's when I stood up and checked my wounds. They were already healing. A couple more minutes and I'd be good as new.

"Says it right here, dude," Mitch whispered. "After the summoning, you must consummate the connection by laying with the summoned."

So that's what they were doing.

I lifted my hands, lighting a couple of flames in each. Like I said, there were certain abilities that hellions had, including the limited summoning of dark energies. I would never even attempt battling an actual magic user with my abilities, though. Even a neophyte mage could end me if we dueled with magic alone.

"You boys got the wrong girl," I said coolly.

"Dude," Mitch whimpered, "she can do magic."

Billy swallowed hard. "I think I'm in love."

There was a thump near the window I'd flown through moments before. A hand gripped the edge. I rushed over and crushed it under my boot. What followed was a yelp, a scream, and a crashing sound.

There was no way the fall had killed Moloch's lackey, but I doubted he was feeling very cozy at the moment.

"I'm definitely in love," Billy confirmed.

"Uh huh," agreed Mitch.

I snapped my fingers at them, which should have

brought them to their senses, but it only seemed to make their eyes melt more.

"Look, idiots," I snarled, "I don't know what kind of game you think you're playing here, but you're about to..." I paused and studied them a little more. Something was definitely off about these two, but I couldn't tell what it was exactly. "Wait, are you two supernaturals?"

"Huh?" they said in unison.

So, no.

But what *was* it with...

Ah, they were normals. Yes, I saw the gangbangers who were likely also normals, but there was too much going on at the time to really study them. Mitch and Billy were the first normals I'd ever gotten a decent look at.

I suddenly had a sour feeling.

If all normals looked like these two, it was going to be a long stay topside.

"What's with the books?" I asked.

"We found them," Mitch answered. "There was some old guy a couple floors up. He was always lugging them around, but—"

"Shut up, Mitch," Billy said, his face the picture of worry.

"Why? She's our property now." He poked at the book. "Says so right here. Well, after we lay—"

"Nobody is laying with me," I interrupted as I walked over and snapped up one of the tomes.

It was old and worn, looking as though it had been around for hundreds of years. The title was *Summonings* by M.W. Hastings. Yep, definitely an old book. One of the originals, if I recalled correctly. Part of being a Guard was knowing a lot about history. Garrick had always said that the more we knew about the past, the more likely we'd know how to defeat the idiots who attempted to repeat it.

I cracked the book back open to where the boys had been working.

Summoning a Succubus was the heading on the page.

Oh boy.

"All right, guys," I said, knowing that Moloch was certainly in search of another way to get to me, "here's the deal. You're playing with things that you think you can control, but you can't. These are nothing but words that you'll never be able to do more than read and recite. You don't have the power needed for this."

They looked at their hands.

"Also," I added, "you may *think* you want a succubus to enter your life, but you don't. She'll drain every ounce of..." I paused, noting their dreamy eyes. "Right. Well, trust me in that you don't want a succubus in your life."

Billy raised his hand.

"Yes?"

"I hear what you're saying and all," he stammered, "but you arrived like two seconds after we'd finished doing the ritual that it said we had to do."

"And we'll probably finish like two seconds after we start the laying with you part," added Mitch.

I squinted at him.

"Ew."

That's when I heard the pounding of footsteps running down the hallway.

Closing my eyes, I focused in on the sound. There was only one set of boots. So either Moloch had split up his attack or he assumed that only one assassin would be needed to kill me.

Some people never learn.

"Get in the bedroom," I commanded the two boys. "Right now!"

They both glanced at each other, smiled enormously, and then stared back at me with a mixture of hope and worry.

Ugh.

"Go!"

They jumped up and ran into the bedroom.

I walked behind them, pulled the door shut, summoned some flame, and melted the handle. They wouldn't be getting out of there anytime soon.

"Stay in there for fifteen minutes or I'll kill you both," I warned.

There was no response.

That probably had to do with them being too busy disrobing, but I really didn't want to think about that at the moment.

I ran back to the window and looked down.

Moloch was walking back and forth, his blades out and ready. I'd been right, but with just him and his goons, that would mean that only two were in the building. He was covering the back and the other was likely around front, or wherever the exit was. Then again, if he was smart, he'd have put one on the roof. I would have. But that would mean only one of them could storm the building in search of me. The single set of boots pounding made me think that was indeed the case.

Okay, so maybe Moloch wasn't as big of a moron as I'd thought.

I turned just as the front door to the apartment got kicked in.

It was the guy I'd booted in the nuts earlier.

He didn't look happy.

"Hey, asshole," I teased, slowly pulling out my blades. "How are the marbles?"

CHAPTER 5

When in doubt, play dirty.

— GARRICK - HOUSE OF SINISTER

*A*sshole roared as he charged me, bringing his blade in for a cut. He'd obviously not been given the lesson regarding the finer points of the arc, though, because he wavered.

I stepped slightly to the side and sliced across his chest as we slid by each other.

When I spun back toward him, I was surprised to see that he was set and ready for another volley. His jacket had a nice set of perfectly angled lines on them, but there was no blood. Come to think of it, his back hadn't bled when I'd sliced him on the street either.

"Armor?" I asked.

"Of course, you slut," he hissed in response.

"Slut?" I laughed. Then I stopped laughing and squinted at him. "Wait, do I know you?"

He dove in again.

He also wavered again.

I stepped off, angled in the opposite direction as he bellowed in rage. He was clearly used to winning his battles quickly. To be fair, he *was* pretty fast. He was also decent with the blade, but there was that split second of a slowdown that was going to kill him.

"Look, Asshole," I said, keeping my blades up, "you're not going to be able to beat me. Trust me, I know. I've fought way too many people at your skill level."

"Save your words, bitch."

"And what's with the name calling?"

He glared at me. "You've been calling me an 'asshole.'"

"That's not me calling you names," I replied, giving him a look. "That's just how I know you." Then I channeled Garrick and a few pixies I knew. "If I was calling you names, it would be something different each time, like Cock Serenader or Jizz Tick."

Anything to put your opponent off balance.

He furrowed his brow. "Jizz Tick?"

This one was a real caveman.

"Okay, okay," I said, waving my blades in the air. "What's your actual name?"

"Welton," he said.

"Welton?" I snorted, but quickly regained control of myself. "Sorry. Welton? Right. Okay...Welton, you don't have a chance against me."

He looked unsure.

"It's not that you're a bad fighter," I explained. "It's just that you're not a great one. You see, I've fought the best of the best. You waver. That'll kill you every time against someone who doesn't waver." I gave him a conspiratorial look. "That'd be me, in case you're still kind of lost with all that I'm saying here."

His eyes grew dark.

"I don't have time for this, whore."

He charged again, bringing his attack from overhead this time. I fell backwards, rolling with his momentum and kicking at the last second so that he flew and crashed into the door where the two teenage boys were awaiting their playdate.

I miscalculated on one thing, though. I hadn't expected the door to break down.

Welton stood up and shook his head, looking like he was trying to clear the cobwebs. At least there was blood this time.

Thankfully, Mitch and Billy were still in their robes. I really had no interest in seeing them otherwise.

Unfortunately, Billy had the look on his face of a guy who thought it was his duty to protect his girl.

"Hey," he said, causing Welton to spin.

Billy moved behind Mitch.

"What the fuck, dude?" Mitch yelped, pushing away from his friend.

Welton's hand gripped his blade tighter. "Who are you two dickheads?"

So much for playing nice-nice with Welton.

I was not at all fond of the fact that Billy and Mitch had been trying to summon a succubus, but those two idiots would have been toast in seconds if I hadn't intervened, and they would have no chance against the likes of Welton.

"Are you planning to touch them inappropriately or something, Welton?" I asked from behind him. "I'm assuming they're old enough where they can offer their own consent, but—"

"Silence!" Welton yelled in response. "It's time for you to die, you c—"

"Do *not* use that word with me, Welton," I warned as I let my energy flow. "I'll tolerate being called a whore and slut, but we keep the c-word out of things."

"The word 'concubine' bothers you that much, does it?"

Actually, it *did*, but that wasn't the word I'd thought he was saying.

He didn't wait for my reply, though. Instead, he did the same style of charging he'd done before. He was incredibly predictable.

Too bad for him, I was running out of time.

Moving with the grace that came through years of training, my blades sang. They did not waver. There was no wasted motion.

I sliced at his exposed neck, face, and hands.

He was dead before his body even knew it, but I'd angled him in such a way that he'd been launched out the same window I'd come in through.

Welton's corpse was moving with such speed that he landed on the corner of the dumpster below, his body bent at an odd angle as his blood poured onto the street in front of Moloch.

"I hope your other assassins are better than good old Welton," I called down. "If not, this is going to be a short night for you."

"Bitch!"

CHAPTER 6

*I*ncluding help from the flame beast, Moloch was down two goons. My summary dismissal of Welton had to have worried him a little. Then again, hellions weren't exactly known for having much common sense when it came to odds in battle.

Myself included.

Garrick had always been wise about that and he'd *tried* to instill in me a bit of that wisdom. If he hadn't, I would have died back at the House with him. There was no way he could have survived the attack, of course, the numbers were too great, but if he had been on the periphery with me, he'd have run too.

It's difficult for a hellion to run when confronted, especially those of us in the Guard.

Honestly, it was almost painful.

I just had to keep chanting "The House comes first" over and over in my thoughts. Without that, I wouldn't have made it this far.

But the fun wasn't over yet, and it wouldn't be for at least a year.

A creak sounded to my right, and I spun with blades at the ready.

Billy and Mitch stood there, peering through the door to the bedroom, their eyes wide with horror.

Good.

With a sigh, I dropped my swords back into their sheaths and dismissed them.

"Hopefully you two have learned a lesson here," I admonished the boys as I pointed at their books. No, they couldn't actually summon anything, and I knew that they hadn't summoned me, but it was obvious their heads were still not sold on that point. "Magic is not something to trifle with. I'm telling you right now that both of you should be dead. If I hadn't been here to dispatch Welton," I added pointing out the window, "he would have cut you to ribbons."

The terror on their faces told me that I'd at least given them something to think about.

Just to drive the point home and add to their fear, I pushed a little more. "If I were you, I'd take these books and burn them. The last thing you want is for an actual wizard, especially the guy who dropped them, to learn that these have fallen into the wrong hands. If that happens, you'll be wishing that Welton *had* cut you to ribbons."

With that, I turned and walked out through the door that Welton had busted down.

I couldn't control what Mitch and Billy chose to do, obviously, and I hadn't the time to hold their hands, and I certainly *wasn't* going to lay with them. Hopefully they'd let the events of the night sink in and burn those books, or carefully return them. If they didn't, they'd be risking some pretty bad shit happening.

But they weren't my problem anymore and it was time for me to put them behind me.

The hallway was clear.

To the left was what appeared to be an elevator. To the right was a flight of stairs.

If I headed down, I'd be greeted by Moloch and another of his goons. If I went up, I'd only have to face one of them.

Fortunately, there was a third option.

I summoned a bit of dark energy and put my hand on the doorknob of the adjacent apartment. It clicked and I gingerly opened it.

The room was dark and quiet. It was sparsely furnished, too, which meant that I would be able to slip through it without making too much noise. Just in case, I opened my senses a bit more.

Nobody home.

Good.

I closed the door gently and tiptoed across the room until I got to the window.

Unlike the apartment that Billy and Mitch were in, this one was almost within touching distance of the building next to it. Plus, it had a pipe that was running from the roof down to the ground. I could use that to scale in either direction. Same problem, though. If I went either up or down there'd be a goon to spot me.

The guy on the roof wouldn't be expecting me to launch in from the other building, though.

Hopefully.

I could climb and either sneak away, or I could better my odds of survival even more by taking down another of Moloch's men.

It'd be just like when I'd killed a sentry from House Mal back in my cadet days, except this guy wouldn't be on a horse and I wouldn't be throwing him back to Moloch. I had no problem doing that with Welton, but it wasn't like I was going to go out of my way to give up my position.

I crouched on the ledge of the window, looking down to make sure the coast was clear. While I had no intention of missing my jump, I wasn't foolish enough to not think of contingencies.

As expected, the second lackey was patrolling below.

I waited until he reached the end of the building and turned before I made my leap.

It wasn't exactly graceful, but I caught the pipe on the other building and waited a few seconds before climbing.

Before long, I was at the top of the building.

I hadn't climbed over the edge yet, though, because I wanted to get a good look at Moloch's other goon.

He was facing the doorway that allowed access to the roof. His crossbow was in hand and he was patiently standing there with it pointed at the door. Clearly he'd planned to release the arrow the moment the door opened, and he probably wouldn't have even bothered to verify it was me before doing it. If some poor sucker happened to go up on the roof for whatever reason, it'd be the last thing they did.

This left me an option, though.

I could take off right now, darting across the top of the roof of the building I was on and slip away into the night. They'd sense I was on the move, eventually, but it'd take a minute or so.

It was the smart move.

"There!" yelled the voice of the assassin below.

The soldier on the opposite roof spun and spotted me as well.

"Fuck," I hissed as I pulled myself over the lip of the building, dropping flat on my back as an arrow sailed overhead.

So much for slipping away into the night.

CHAPTER 7

There's always a way out, it just may be through death.

— GARRICK - HOUSE OF SINISTER

I was running, jumping, zigging, and zagging as crossbow boy fired arrow after arrow at me. If he'd had any brains at all, he would have spent more time chasing me and less time loading fresh points.

Just as that thought flooded through my brain, an arrow zipped right past my ear.

That was close.

Too close.

I bolted toward the access door on the next building, pulled it open, and rushed inside.

There was a *thud* sound that told me I'd opened the door just in time. Glancing back, I saw the tip of an arrow poking through.

Just as I was about to speed down the stairs, I paused and thought there was a better way to handle this.

"She just took the access door down," I heard Captain Crossbow yelling. "Want me to chase her and you come up the other way?"

I summoned my blades, but only removed one, hoping that Moloch had agreed with the plan.

The instant crossbow boy yanked open the door, I stepped up and slid the sword into his throat. The look on his face registered both shock and pain. That worked for me, considering how he'd been trying to pierce my brain for the last couple of minutes.

As he gurgled his last breath, I stepped forward and kicked him in the chest, allowing him to slide off my blade and fall flat on his back. Then, I leaned down and wiped his blood off the weapon, using his jacket, as I looked him in his dying eyes.

"Thanks for the idea about just standing at the door and waiting," I said. "It's kind of cowardly, but I figured if it was a good enough way for you to kill, it'd be a good enough way for you to die."

…and die he did.

I returned my sword and looked out over the city.

Again, going toward the lights seemed to be my gut instinct. If nothing else, there'd be tons of people there and that meant I could try to get lost in the crowd.

It wouldn't be easy to do though, because hellions could find other hellions. That wasn't managed through sight or smell or even feel. It was something beyond that. Almost a form of magnetism. It was an active skill, though, taking focus or at least years of practice to manage it passively. But those who were good at the practice of sniffing out other hellions, were also pretty good at hiding themselves.

As a Guard, I was able to tune in quite nicely.

I was also able to hide, just not easily against people who were well-versed in tracking.

Something told me that Moloch and his crew were also rather adept at that skill when they wanted to be. If they hadn't been, I would have sensed them long before they hit the landing back at the House during the Rite of Decimation. To be fair to me, though, I had been watching my teacher fighting for his life.

I hopped the lip on the next two buildings, running toward the mass of city lights. When I hit the edge of the next building in line, I parkoured my way down through a series of smaller rooftops until I hit the pavement.

Moloch and his last remaining assassin were on their way, too. That only served to confirm that they were both as capable of tracking as I was.

Super.

I judged the major population to be only a couple miles away, which was nothing for me. Garrick had us running constantly during our incessant training. Not that I was complaining. I loved to train. It was the next best thing to actual battle.

When I finally got to the main area, I found there'd been a pretty heavy vehicle pileup. Only a few people ran in to help out as others just stood there staring.

Based on the tone of the crowd, it was clear that there were some bodies in those cars that hadn't made it.

That would work out perfectly for me, if I could find the right person to inhabit who had already died. But I'd have to choose carefully so that Moloch wouldn't just come in and start ripping apart the dead. Another look around told me that not even he was stupid enough to do that with all these people around. There were certainly at least *some* supernaturals here, meaning that they'd step up and fight. Not that they'd have much of a chance against a couple of hellions, but, again, strength in numbers.

Speaking of Moloch, I could feel he was getting closer. I couldn't pinpoint him, but he and his buddy were definitely closing in.

It was time to act.

I darted around the outer edge of the crowd until I circled around to come up on the other side of the wreck. There were fewer people over here, meaning that I was able to have at least a little cover as I sought out a body to inhabit.

Getting in sooner was better than later.

Obviously, I could have just jumped into someone from the crowd, but I was thinking longer term than that.

I was stuck topside for a year.

If there was a recently deceased among this bunch of unfortunates, I'd rather just take over and live their life for a while.

That's when I spotted the white stretch limousine.

A quick scan of the area told me that the people here were upperclass. The clothes, the hair, the shoes, and the rest were all things that screamed wealth. I wasn't one who'd been raised with all the finer things. If push came to shove, I'd rather drop back a few shots of whiskey over having a drink with an umbrella in it. Honestly, I didn't know if that's what wealthy people did or not, but it seemed to be the common stereotype among the Guard.

The back door of the limo was hanging open on this side, so I quickly peered in.

She was the only inhabitant and she was lying facedown on the floor, between the rows of seats. Either she was going to pick up others to fill this massive ride or she was just generally wealthy.

I reached out to feel if she was still alive, which was precisely when I felt her give up the ghost.

Too bad for her, but perfect timing for me.

At least she was going to the Vortex.

The pull of Moloch struck me, telling me that he'd just reached the area.

It was time to take over Miss Moneybags.

CHAPTER 8

The sound of sirens filled the air as I took over the body. Emergency personnel would push Moloch back even further, especially if there were any Paranormal Police Department officers nearby. While standard supernaturals would struggle against Moloch and his assassin pal, PPD cops had a little extra something in the tank. They'd still have the cards stacked against them in a one-on-one battle, but Moloch would be on the losing end if he was facing a gang of them.

I took a quick inventory of the body I was in. She was dead, so it was a little tough to get a full reading on things, but I pushed myself until I had enough to go on. The worst case scenario was that the body was so fucked up that I couldn't do anything to get it functioning again.

Her wrist was broken, as was her collarbone and a few ribs. One of the ribs had punctured a lung. That couldn't have felt very good. She had a nice bruise on her right cheek, but her head was otherwise in decent shape. I'd been worried that there might be brain damage.

But what was it that killed her?

It could have been the collapsed lung, mixed with the shock and pain of the entire ordeal.

I checked the heart next and found the source of the problem. I was no doctor, but even I could see there was a thickness to the muscle that seemed wrong. The jolt of adrenaline most likely put her over the top and her body couldn't cope.

Fortunately, one of the awesome things about bodily possession was the ability to alter and repair the one who was being possessed. I didn't want to do anything specific to the heart without first understanding the depth of how normals differed from hellions, but I could at least send through a spark to get things rolling again.

It took two shocks, but it worked.

The heart started up.

There was no chance that the previous owner was going to return, but that just meant I'd be able to live her life for her.

At least for a while.

After a quick repair on the lung and ribs, I reached over with my good arm and grabbed her purse. I didn't want to fix all of my injuries as that would have looked a little too perfect.

Her name was Evelyn Grayson. That worked out since being called "Eve" would be perfect. If she had any friends or family who called her by her full name, though, that'd take some getting used to. Oh well, better that than dead. Also, in the purse was a note of thanks from the Children's Cancer Center of Greater Los Angeles and a ticket to an art exhibit tonight.

"I'll check the limo and you get the cab," called out a man's voice.

I quickly stuffed the contents of the purse back into place and pushed it away from me, closing my eyes and groaning slightly.

The vehicle rocked as the whoosh of sounds came in.

"Ma'am," the guy said, "I'm a paramedic. Can you hear me?"

I groaned lightly in response.

"Can you tell me where it hurts, ma'am?"

Technically, it didn't hurt, which was probably an issue. If I was to pull off this ruse, I needed to fully integrate with this body.

Ugh.

It took a few seconds for the connection to complete, but it took no time for the pain to rake through my body.

And that let me know that the one place I hadn't checked was Evelyn's legs.

Apparently, there was a compound break on the fibula. *My* fibula.

I'd have to quit thinking of this body in the third-person.

The pain helped.

"Fuck," I hissed.

"Try to stay as still as possible, ma'am," the paramedic said. "Do you have any allergies?"

How the hell should I know?

"No," I grunted.

If my new body *did* have an allergy, I'd just fix it. If I couldn't, I'd become a male paramedic because I'd just jump from Grayson to the guy trying to help me. Yes, I knew that taking over a live body in any permanent fashion was deemed a Voidable offense, but I was beyond giving a shit at this point.

"I'm going to give you a painkiller, ma'am."

I moaned my approval.

Then, I disconnected from the pain receptors. I had enough to go on to fake it from here.

"How is she?" asked a female voice from the other side of the door.

"Working on her," the guy answered.

That's when I heard Moloch. I couldn't feel him while possessing the body and I knew he couldn't sense me either, but his voice was unmistakable.

"She could be in there," he was saying, standing just within earshot.

"Do you really think she'd pick a wealthy person?" asked Moloch's goon.

"Ma'am," the paramedic said, grabbing Grayson's purse, "do you know your name?"

I coughed a couple of times for show and then said, "Eve Grayson."

"Yep," said the female paramedic. "That's right. Her name is Evelyn Grayson." She paused. "Hey, wait, isn't she the one who just gave a ton of money to charity the other day?"

"I don't know," the guy replied.

"Yes," I rasped. "The Children's Cancer Center of Greater Los Angeles."

"What did she say?" asked the woman.

"Children's Cancer Center in L.A.," the guy replied.

"Yep, that's her alright. Treat her well, Dale. She's a good one."

"I treat them all well, Alice," he grumbled.

"Damn it," Moloch cursed. "She couldn't have known that information. You search that way and I'll go the other. My guess is that she knew we'd be hunting for her here and so she jumped into another body and got out."

"Agreed."

"Check them all anyway," commanded Moloch.

I breathed a sigh of relief.

I'd gotten away for now. There was still a long time ahead of me, but as long as I kept the body of Evelyn Grayson functioning and learned to play her role properly, I might just make it.

At least through the night.

CHAPTER 9

*T*hey weren't precisely seated in the same room. That would be too dangerous. Instead, they were using a form of technology that allowed them to project themselves bodily into a selected room that had been configured for them.

Even then, though, they went to great lengths to ensure that they could not be seen by each other or anyone else.

Security protocols were exceedingly important at this level of life. People of lower stations, even those who were among the top three percent in wealth and power, were not as important as the members here. This was especially true from the point of view of the members here.

They were the one percent.

Not the entirety of the one percent, obviously, but three of them who had decided to work together for a common purpose.

It was against the standard conduct for members of the one percent to collaborate this closely on matters, but

Leighton, Simone, and Abner felt it was paramount that they do so. If they failed, war would eventually strike.

"I think she will suffice for our purposes," Leighton stated.

"Perfectly," agreed Simone.

Abner was the least vocal of them all, but even his grunted opinion on the matter was positive.

The air stood still in the room as the three watched the live feed of the last member of House Sinister as she was loaded into an ambulance and taken to a local hospital.

It wasn't her body, but those in the one percent could see more than most.

"And Moloch?" asked Simone. "What shall we do with him?"

"Let him continue his search," Leighton replied. "He'll fail eventually."

"Which means he'll be executed," Simone stated.

"Precisely."

Nobody seemed bothered by that likely eventuality. Then again, why would they be? Anyone not in their station was nothing more than a tool for them to use in any way they deemed necessary. A carpenter may have a favorite hammer, but even that will eventually be replaced when one more suitable for the job comes along.

"What's the plan with her?" Abner asked, his voice gruff and pained.

"Same as the others," Leighton answered. "We'll send Kayson and Quinton down to bring her into the fold."

CHAPTER 10

If the opportunity for vengeance presents itself, tread carefully. Always take the opportunity, obviously, just don't be a dumbass about it.

— GARRICK - HOUSE OF SINISTER

I woke up to find myself in what looked like a hospital room. I knew I'd been pretty exhausted, but I hadn't expected to crash like that.

Then it hit me. I was connected to a body that had been massively drugged.

Damn it.

My wrist and leg had both healed, but I still had a bandage on my face. At least the bandage would make my story more believable if Moloch had decided to follow-up on Evelyn Grayson's story. I'm not sure how I would be able to explain away the instant healing of bones, though.

But all of that didn't worry me nearly as much as seeing that there were two men in the room with me, and they were most certainly *not* doctors. They also weren't hellions. If they were, I'd have been dead already.

"She's awake, Q," the taller of the two said.

He was incredibly attractive. Long, black hair, tanned features, eyes that had no business being that green, and he was clearly built. I would have placed him as being a vampire, but something told me he wasn't one. It was probably the outfit. It looked too rogue, especially with the layering of shirts.

"I can see that, Kayson," replied the smaller man, who wasn't exactly what I'd call unattractive, but there was something about him that made me instantly uncomfortable. It was probably that he was *too* perfect. His clothes were flawlessly pressed, his hair was slicked back with precision, and his eyes were the kind that sought out imperfections. "Please allow me to do the talking?"

"Whatever, dude," Kayson replied with a roll of his eyes.

I wanted to just jump in and ask who they were and what they wanted, but Garrick hadn't trained a fool. I'd speak when I was prepared.

"Your name?" asked Q.

I didn't reply.

"Listen, girl," he said with some heat, "I have very little patience for someone who—"

"All right, all right," Kayson said, stepping over and pushing Q out of the way. "Chill out, Q. The lady's been banged up pretty bad, you know?"

Good cop, bad cop?

"Sorry about that," Kayson said. "He's just kind of a dick."

"I beg your pardon?"

Kayson raised his eyebrows at me. "See?" He sat on the edge of the bed and eyed me. "I'm Kayson and that's Quinton, but I call him Q because it irritates him."

Q harrumphed.

"Anyway, we're Black Ops," Kayson continued. "We take out assholes and such."

Was I considered an asshole?

I almost laughed at my own thought. The fact was that I *was* an asshole, most of the time anyway. But, again, I doubted these guys were sent here to wait for me to wake up so they could kill me.

Unless, of course, they were going to verify who I was first.

"See," Kayson said, "we already know who you are."

"Evangeline of the House of Sinister," announced Q.

I flinched slightly at that.

Kayson winked at me. "Don't worry. We're not telling anyone."

Okay, so they knew who I was, and even if they hadn't, I'd just done a decent enough job of giving it away. Yet, here I sat, still breathing.

"What do you want?" I asked, finally.

Q stepped over and folded his arms. "For reasons that were not divulged to me, you have been selected to join us."

"Join you?"

"Yeah," Kayson said. "The big boys want you working for Black Ops, too."

I had no idea what he was talking about, but I assumed it had something to do with covert operations of some sort. Either that, or it was an elaborate plan for getting me to follow them somewhere that they could kill me without it being traced.

No, that was dumb, and more than just a bit paranoid.

If I was killed inside this body, it would happen without the standard medical community having a clue. Their autopsy wouldn't turn up anything.

They weren't planning to kill me.

Not here, anyway.

"What does working for Black Ops mean?" I ventured.

"Oh, it's great," answered Kayson, his perfect smile lighting up the room. "We kill assholes, like I said before. Plus, we steal intel, fuck up people's plans, play the spy game, and a bunch of other shit."

There wasn't any way to tell if these guys were for real or not, but Kayson seemed to genuinely love his job. My gut told me all was clear, though, and seeing that Garrick put a lot of stock in gut-reactions, I decided to play along.

It wasn't as if I'd had much of a choice anyway.

Besides, if they were for real, I may just get the chance to kill off some members from the Houses of Varaz, Mathen, and Tross.

That wouldn't suck.

"Do you assassinate hellions?" I asked.

"Of course," answered Q.

"I'm in," I replied without hesitation as I pushed myself up.

The pain receptors were connected in full. I shut them back off and caught my breath.

"Is this your first possession?" asked Q, clearly enjoying the fact that I was in some discomfort.

"Full one, yes," I admitted, and then looked at Kayson. "Is he always this fun?"

Kayson nodded. "Yup."

"Yay," I said, rolling my eyes. "So...now what?"

"Now," Q replied, "you go back and live the life you stole from whomever this body belongs to."

"I didn't steal the body. She was—"

"You're wasting your breath," interrupted Kayson. "He doesn't give a shit."

Q shot Kayson a look, but then slowly nodded his head. "True."

Then Q pulled out a syringe, flicked the needle, and then shoved it unceremoniously into my arm. Fortunately, I'd disconnected from the pain or that would have hurt a fair bit. It was a rather large needle and Q was *not* being gentle with it.

"There," stated Q, tucking the syringe back into his jacket.

I glanced down at my arm. "There, what?"

"I've finished," he replied, as if I were stupid.

"I got that, dipshit," I snapped. "What I'm asking is what the hell did you just finish doing?"

Q squinted at me. "I just finished giving you the tattoo and your personal connector."

"Bah," Kayson jumped in again. "Ignore him. He's a dick funnel. The tattoo lets you do a bunch of shit. You can transport to base, you can do some minor healing on yourself, you can hack it to give you the best orgasm you've ever had..."

He looked away wistfully.

"You're not supposed to use PPD property for anything it isn't intended for," Q chastised him.

"Perks is perks," Kayson stated with a shrug. "Q's just a prude."

"I most certainly am *not*," Q argued. "It's just that—"

"Wait," I said, after filing away that orgasm comment, just in case, "this is a PPD thing? As in the Paranormal Police Department?"

"Yup," Kayson replied.

"Obviously," Q added.

"Hold on," I said, thinking that made very little sense seeing as how they'd just told me I was an assassin. "I'm a cop now?"

"Yup."

"Not precisely," Q disagreed with Kayson. "You are above the law, yet you are still working for the masters who pull the strings *of* the law."

"Uh huh," I said to him and then looked back at Kayson. "Am I a cop or am I a killer?"

"Yup."

"Both, in a manner of speaking," Q tried again. "There are certain criminal elements that act so far behind the scenes that the standard PPD officers cannot get to them."

"And Black Ops kills them?"

"Yup," Kayson chanted again, though now he was busily cleaning his nails with the blade of a knife.

"We do *not* kill them," moaned Q. "We *assassinate* them."

I furrowed my brow.

"What's the difference?"

"One is honorable."

"Ah," I said, nodding. "Which one?"

Kayson chuckled.

"I think I'm going to like you," he said.

"I think I shall not," Q stated with force.

"Even more reason I will," Kayson laughed.

I wasn't sure how to feel about all this, but if these guys were really going to bring me into the fold of the PPD and allow me to hunt down and kill…or 'assassinate' hellions, that was good enough for me.

CHAPTER 11

*A*doctor I hadn't seen before entered the room. She was tall and beyond beautiful. I couldn't see a single line or blemish on her face or neck. It was as though she were some kind of mannequin. If it hadn't been for the white lab coat she was wearing, I'd have thought that a supermodel had walked into the wrong room.

"Gentlemen," she said to Kayson and Q as if she knew them both.

"What's up, Doc?" Kayson replied in his best Bugs Bunny voice.

"Doctor Gillian," Q said more formally, adding a bow. "Always a pleasure."

I glanced at Kayson. He wiggled his eyebrows at me and nodded, affirming my suspicion that Q had a thing for the doctor.

That also meant that she wasn't your standard, everyday doctor. She must have worked for the PPD, also. Or, if she didn't, she at least knew about it. But why would a doctor work for a group of assassins? I suppose it could have been that she thought that Black Ops was just an elite group of cops and didn't know about the killing-people part.

"What happened to my other doctors?" I ventured.

"They've been reassigned," she replied with a perfect smile as she placed a device near my new ink. "I'll be your doctor going forward."

"She's excellent," Q breathed.

"Thank you, Quinton," Dr. Gillian replied, giving him a casual grin.

That prompted another knowing wink from Kayson.

"It seems that your tattoo is fully integrated," she announced a few moments later. Then, she glanced up at me in surprise. "A hellion? Impressive."

Q sneered, making it clear that he wasn't a fan of hellions.

Kayson shook his head at Q's sneer and then nodded at me as if to say that *he* was cool with hellions.

Of course, that could have been because Kayson was a...

Actually, I didn't know precisely *what* he was, but it was definitely something I'd encountered before. I just couldn't place it.

Demons were pretty decent at hiding, just like hellions. Considering we shared similar ancestry, that made sense. But I'd been around enough of them to know that Kayson was *not* a demon, and he damn sure wasn't a hellion. Werewolf? Maybe. He did fit the profile...sort of.

Dr. Gillian tapped on the device she was holding, bringing my attention back to her.

"Okay," she said, "your connector has been seated, too, but you probably haven't noticed it."

"Seeing as I have no idea what you're talking about, I'd have to agree."

"The connector is a device that is wired to certain areas of your brain," she explained. "It'll allow you to mentally communicate with your team, and anyone else on the authorized list."

I raised my eyebrows at that. "Sounds nifty."

"It is quite impressive, actually," she agreed. "However, since you're not the rightful owner of this body, you may have to connect to it through nonstandard means."

Just as I was about to ask precisely how I would go about doing that, Dr. Gillian put a different device on my chest and began studying it.

"You've already done some repairs on your own, I see," she murmured. "You've got a thickened heart wall there."

"That's what killed her," I replied. "The lady who originally owned this body, I mean."

She nodded distantly. "As good a guess as any." She then moved the device again. "Are you able to thin that wall some? I can tell you when it's at optimal."

"Uh...sure," I replied, glancing over at the two Black Ops fellas. "Give me a sec here."

I focused inward again, like I'd done back at the limo. It took a little longer this time as I was abundantly cognizant of the eyes on me. I'd been rushed back when Moloch and his assassin pal were hot on my trail, but there was something wholly different between being in danger and being watched.

After finally sinking into the moment, I found myself able to control the heart more comfortably.

"Good," said the distant voice of Dr. Gillian. "You want to lessen the thickness by roughly fifty-percent. Slowly, though."

I worked on it for what seemed an eternity before she finally told me that everything was perfect. Just in case, I took a quick peek at the arteries to make sure there wasn't any build up going on.

All good.

When I opened my eyes again, I found that the good doctor had already exited the room.

"Where'd she go?" I asked.

"Attending another *fortunate* soul, no doubt," hummed Q.

"Keep it in your pants, pal," Kayson said. "Vampires and fae don't tend to play nice-nice, remember?"

"There are always exceptions," Q argued gently.

Kayson spun his finger in a circle by his own ear as he leaned his head toward Q.

"You keep telling yourself that," he said with a pinch of sarcasm.

Okay, what the hell was Kayson? It was really getting to me.

Q was obviously a vampire and Dr. Gillian was a fae, but I couldn't...

Sometimes you could just look at the style of a super and know what they were. This was especially true with vampires and fae. The stereotypes about their kind being pompous, snappily dressed, and exacting were on the nose. Fae took it a step further by being incredibly attractive. Not that vampires weren't pleasant to look at, too, but fae brought it to an entirely new level.

Kayson, though, was an anomaly.

He was definitely good-looking, in a roguish sort of way. His choice of garb indicated that he couldn't give two-shits about how people viewed his sense of style. Not that it was bad. It was just very…pirate? No, there wasn't an eyepatch or a billowing shirt, but he *did* have tall black boots on and his shirts were on in layers. It looked so damn familiar, but I just couldn't place it.

"What are you?" I asked with some hesitation. "I mean, I hate to ask, but you're obviously not a vampire or fae. At the same time, you're good-looking."

"I'm liking you more by the minute," he said, flashing his pearly whites.

Q groaned and shook his head.

"Seriously," I said. "Q is obviously a vampire. Dr. Gillian is a fae. You already know that I'm a hellion." I tilted my head at him again. "I'm just having one hell of a time figuring out what race you are."

"Hellwolf," he replied with a slight bow.

The blood drained from my face.

"I thought there were only twenty of you left in existence," I rasped.

"You know about us, eh?" Kayson replied, looking impressed.

I glanced over at Q, who appeared to be contemplating whether or not to go after Dr. Gillian and ask her out.

"*Yes,*" I attempted through the connector. "*Can you hear me okay?*"

"We both can," Q replied aloud. "Glad to see you

figured out how to use your connector, though." I hadn't 'figured' anything out. It just sort of happened. "If you're just trying to speak with Kayson privately, you'll have to set it accordingly."

"Oh."

Well, so much for my attempt at being coy.

"Just imagine the connector as your own personal cell phone and you'll be able to mentally target me," Kayson said.

I did.

"There, I think."

We both looked at Q, but he wasn't paying attention to us.

"Q," I said without changing my connector setting, *"I think Dr. Gillian has the hots for you."*

Kayson snorted. *"No, she doesn't. She thinks he's a wad."* He gave me a grin. *"She's right, too."*

"I was just verifying that he couldn't hear me," I replied. *"Anyway, I was on the team that helped the hellwolves get to Netherworld Proper. Garrick was my mentor."*

The look on Kayson's face changed to one of seriousness.

"Garrick is a good man."

"Yes," I replied, looking off into the distance. *"Unfortunately, he fell tonight in battle. Everyone in my House did. I'm all that remains."*

"Damn." Kayson closed his eyes for a moment. *"Sorry."*

"Yeah."

"Well," he said, after a moment, reopening his glittery greens, *"on the plus side, you're going to get a ton of chances to kill the fuckers who did it."*

"Once you two are done with your secret discussion,"

Q said, turning his attention back to us, "I will signal the nursing staff to take Evelyn Grayson here out of the hospital so she can return home."

"Home?" I said, my eyes wide. "What happened to me joining the Black Ops?"

His look was one of annoyance.

"If you don't show up as Evelyn Grayson, my dear," he said in a patronizing tone, "news will get out about that."

"So?"

"So," he continued, "you didn't exactly choose the body of someone who is beneath the radar, now did you?"

"Still not getting it," I said, chewing my lip.

"Honestly! Eve, you're a hellion inhabiting the body of a normal. That means you're on the run. Any hellion with even half a brain knows that possession of a normal will result in permanent death. Our masters—"

"Jailers," interrupted Kayson.

Q gave him a look and then an agreeing nod.

"They have clearly selected you to serve your penance along with us."

Wait, was Q just declaring that those who were part of Black Ops were serving a sentence of some kind? Were these two criminals or something?

Not that I really gave a shit, but it was nice to know who had your back when doing nefarious things.

"So you're both prisoners?"

"Not really," Kayson answered. "Well, dipshit here is."

Q sighed.

"He embezzled from the one percent like some fucking ass clown." Kayson laughed. "I mean, who does that?"

"Q, apparently," I replied.

"Exactly!" The hellwolf pointed at me. "Anyway, I'm here because I tried to get back into the Badlands after…" he trailed off. "Anyway, that didn't go so well. I barely made it out with my tail between my legs. Tried to go back to Netherworld Proper, but they told me to fuck off." He shrugged. "Can't say I blame them, seeing that the reason I'd tried to get back into the Badlands was to get away from them. I'd kind of built a reputation with the werewolf ladies down there." He gave me a mischievous grin. "Once you go hellwolf, you know what it's like to be fucked."

"Don't I know it," Q muttered.

"What?" Kayson said, grimacing. "You've boned a hellwolf?"

"Ah," Q deadpanned, "you meant fornication."

These two were clearly not the best of friends, but I sensed that there was some form of trust between them otherwise. I'd been down that road before with people I'd fought with. We weren't always the best of friends, but we knew we could trust each other when push came to shove.

"Funny guy," Kayson said, motioning toward Q. "Anyhoo, I escaped topside and was told that if I gave two years to Black Ops, and I didn't fuck up much, I'd be given clearance to return to Netherworld Proper."

"How much time do you have left?" I asked.

"Five years," he said. "I fuck up a lot." His smile came back. "Between you and me, though, I'd be fine staying here. Fun job. I get to kill stuff. I get laid a lot. The food's decent. Plus, I've got a decent place near the beach."

Q kept his gaze steady.

"What about you, Q?" I asked. "How much time do you have left on your sentence?"

"Three hundred twenty-seven days, nineteen hours, thirty-one minutes, and twelve seconds," he replied without hesitation.

Kayson sniffed at that.

"Told you he was anal."

What kind of police department made people join who were serving a sentence? Didn't that kind of go against the purpose of the law? Why would you want the inmates running the asylum?

"Wait," I said, "does everyone in the PPD know about Black Ops?"

"Nope," answered Kayson. "Some do, no doubt, but it being called 'Black Ops' is indicative of the fact that it's to be kept secret."

So Q was anal and Kayson was an asshole.

Got it.

"And they put criminals in positions of power in the PPD?"

"Power?" Q remarked with some derision. "We are pinned by the thumb of the masters. Everything we do is under their scrutiny."

"Q's right," Kayson agreed. "Oh, and always keep in mind that Captain Tattletale here will rat you out if you go against the rules."

I blinked and glanced over at Q.

"To do otherwise," the vampire stated, keeping his eyes glued to mine, "would serve no other purpose than to extend my sentence." He crossed his arms. "I have no desire to serve in this capacity any longer than is absolutely required."

I was learning more and more by the minute. Kayson was a fan of being in Black Ops and Q wasn't.

Fair enough.

Some people had felt that way about serving in the Guard, too. They did their time and got out. I was more like Kayson in that respect, though. Actually, I was probably more like him in many respects.

"I don't suppose you know what my sentence is?" I asked. "Actually, I don't even know what I've done wrong, aside from escape assassination, but seeing that you've just inducted me into service…"

I trailed off as Q and Kayson shared a look.

"That's between you and the masters," Q answered, finally.

"Right. When do I meet them?"

"Soon."

CHAPTER 12

$\mathcal{I}$ was wheeled out of the hospital by a nurse who was as perfect as Dr. Gillian. Apparently, the fae had cornered the Black Ops healthcare market.

There was a white limo waiting for me, along with a woman wearing a smart suit and cap. My assumption was that she was my driver, but the wisps of crimson hair, sparkling blue eyes, and a body that said she was likely into lifting weights told me she was capable of more than getting from point A to point B.

On top of that, I sensed she was a shifter of some sort.

"I hope you are feeling better, ma'am," the woman said. "I'm sorry to inform you that Chaps did not survive the accident."

Recalling that the only other person in the limo was the driver, I assumed that had been Chaps.

"That's terrible," I rasped, doing my best to appear distraught.

There was no way for me to know if she knew him or not, but I was certain that the original owner of this body at least knew who the guy was. Then again, I knew a number of wealthy types in the Badlands who wouldn't remember my name three seconds after I'd given it to them, and many of those I'd worked with on protection duty for years.

Now, I couldn't say if Grayson's relationship with Chaps was good, bad, or indifferent, but my response seemed appropriate.

After feeding me into the car, the driver moved to the front and pulled out of the hospital.

It was light out now, though a bit smoggy. The area was nice enough. Small buildings surrounded us, along with some trees, a few of which looked odd. They were tall and thin with strange leaves at the top. There were also a number of pedestrians, cars, and motorcycles. I guessed that horses weren't as common up here as they were in certain areas of hellion territory.

"Well done, ma'am," the driver said, rolling down the privacy window. "I wasn't sure if there was anyone around who may have been looking for you, so I'm glad you played along."

I furrowed my brow. "I'm sorry?"

"The name is Rainey," she stated. "I was assigned to you from BOPPD."

"Sorry, the bopped?"

"Black Ops PPD."

"Oh, BOPPD," I replied, thinking it sounded funny.

Assigned to me or not, I couldn't trust this person any more than I could trust anyone at this point. I didn't have much of a choice with Kayson and Q. At least for now, everyone had to be a suspect or I'd be dead and the House of Sinister would be permanently gone.

I flicked my thoughts to my dual blades, summoning them ever-so-slightly. I didn't want them to appear, but I needed to know that they would if I truly needed them.

The light pressure of them crossing my back was reassuring.

I dismissed them immediately.

"What do you know exactly?" I asked Rainey.

"Just that you work for Black Ops, ma'am," she answered. "I'm not given any deeper details into any of my assignments, and I'm absolutely fine with that. The less we all know about each other, the better."

There was no arguing with that.

One of Garrick's longstanding rules was that the Guard never visited each other's homes. We could all go out as a team to get shitfaced, pair up for a raid on a neighboring House, and even rut with each other at a hotel or whatever, but we never got too personal.

Of course, that had more to do with the fact that of all the people a hellion could trust, another hellion was the least of them.

That felt a little unfair seeing as Garrick was someone I had trusted implicitly.

He'd sworn that was a different thing, claiming it had to do with a soldier's bond. When we were on the field, we were only as safe as the eyes watching our backs. If you couldn't trust that person, they couldn't trust you either, which put you both in harm's way.

Ultimately, what he'd really meant about getting too close was that you had to be careful not to play favorites.

If we were attacked, each of us had to protect those who were most likely to survive. Relationships that ran too deep colored the ability to make hard choices when blades and bullets were involved.

"You're a shifter, no?" I ventured.

"Again, ma'am," she replied, staring at me in the rearview mirror, "the less we know about each other, the better."

"Right."

It was worth a shot.

Still, I could tell that she was a shifter. It was obvious in the way she moved. I had no idea what kind, though. Not that it really mattered. I just liked to know who I was dealing with at all times, whenever possible.

"Okay, well we both know that we're both part of the Paranormal Police Department, right?"

"Yes, ma'am," she answered. "There's nothing wrong with us being privy to that bit of knowledge."

"So what can you tell me about the PPD that I should know, Rainey?"

She glanced back at me in the rearview mirror for a moment. The look in her eyes told me that I should at least know *something* about the PPD.

"I mean," I said quickly, "I know what the PPD is and such, but I've never been an officer. Based on the little you've told me, you've been on multiple assignments and I'm simply the latest."

"Yes, ma'am," her response was somewhat curt, sounding as if she was almost chastising herself for giving away even that minute amount of data.

I glanced out the window as a blue and black motorcycle zipped past.

"So," I continued, "here I am, a new cop on the force. I have a basic idea of what that means due to the information that..." I paused. "Well, let's just say that I understand the basics of my role on the force. What I don't understand is how do I get back and forth to base? For that matter, where is the base? Who is my boss? Do I get a uniform, a gun, and a badge, or what?"

Rainey was nodding as I continued my tirade.

I didn't know if she'd been down this road before with new people who'd been brought into Black Ops or not, but I couldn't imagine any other reason she'd been 'assigned' to me.

"Yes, ma'am," she replied, sounding upbeat again. "Your tattoo has been configured to allow you immediate transport to home base. This is done via your connector, but I ask you not to activate it just yet. In fact, it's best that you not portal out from your house at all, if you can avoid it."

"I wouldn't even know how," I sighed.

"I've been tasked with getting you home so that your staff can see that Miss Grayson is alive and well."

That was another problem. *I* wasn't Miss Grayson. I was just a hellion who was inhabiting her body.

Translation: How was I supposed to act around these people?

Was Grayson nice to her crew? Was she aloof? Was she a downright bitch?

"Speaking of Grayson," I said, "I don't suppose you have any idea what kind of person she was?"

"Not a clue, ma'am," Rainey replied, "but I'm doing a bunch of studying on her to figure as much out as I can. So far I'd guess she was a narcissistic bitch, based on the few interviews I'd seen with her, but that could have been all for show."

I furrowed my brow at that. "I thought she was heavily into philanthropy?"

"Yes, ma'am," Rainy said. "She was also one of those who dealt in art, politics, and business ventures that only the financially elite could manage." She looked up into the mirror. "Ma'am, you didn't just pick someone with money to inhabit. You chose one of the wealthiest women in the world."

First off, yay. I mean, it was great that I was loaded for once in my life. Having tons of coin was not something I was used to, though, and that meant I'd be fucking up more often than not as I got the hang of things. Secondly, I despised people who felt they were above others. To be fair, I *was* a hellion, which meant that it was fundamental knowledge we were better than everyone else, but I mean within a certain sect. Third, Rainey clearly knew that I was inhabiting the body of a normal, which implied that she also knew I was either a hellion or a demon. My guess was she suspected me to be a demon since hellions coming topside was unheard of.

"Any recommendations on how I should act around everyone?" I asked, not really expecting an answer.

"Selective amnesia?" she suggested.

Not a bad idea.

CHAPTER 13

The world is separated into multiple classes. If you have to ask to which you belong, it's one of the lower ones.

— GARRICK - HOUSE OF SINISTER

*W*e pulled through a large set of gates that were manned by soldiers on either side. They looked to be normals, which wouldn't do anything to stop Moloch, should he find me. The long driveway ended at the front door of a mansion that could have been used for the set of Demented Abbey, a hellion television show that depicted the fictional lives of servants a hundred years ago. I'd never gotten into the show, personally, but it was one of Garrick's strange vices.

"You going to be okay, ma'am?" Rainey asked before getting out of the vehicle.

"Probably not," I answered honestly. "I just need a little time."

"Well, that's likely what the PTB will give you," she laughed. "A little time. *Very* little."

"PTB?"

"Powers That Be," she explained as she turned the wheel to bring me to the front door where a bunch of maids and butlers stood. "Show time, ma'am."

She exited the limo and walked to the passenger side as I looked out at the faces of butlers and maids. These were the 'help' for Evelyn Grayson. Their faces were grim, but I couldn't tell if that was due to concern about the wellbeing of their boss or if they were displeased that she'd survived the accident at all.

I chose to believe the former.

"Our hearts mourn during these tragic events, Miss Grayson," the butler said, his face downcast. He was older with gray hair, a firm look, dull eyes, and taut skin. My first thought was that he was a vampire, but it was difficult to imagine a vampire playing the role of butler. Then again, maybe he was just a normal? Honestly, I may have been looking for things that just weren't there at this point. "Mr. Morrison was a gentleman, madam."

Morrison? Ah, that must have been the last name of the limo driver.

"I'm sorry," I said, "but my memory is a bit sketchy." I paused and glanced around. "I see flashes of recollection, and I know my name and some basic details about myself, but the rest is like a dream that you just can't remember. Mr. Morrison?"

"Your driver, madam," the butler replied.

"Oh," I said, feigning sadness. "Yes. I'm sure he was a wonderful person."

"My name is Baldrick, madam," he added with a hopeful look in his eye. "I'd wished you would have recalled, but I can see that you are truly lost."

I dropped my head and wiped my eyes as he led me into the house, each member of the staff following except for Rainey.

"I'm sorry," I said, throwing in a healthy dose of drama before looking up and around at long faces in the room with me. "I'm truly sorry, but I don't remember any of you."

My next thought was to break down and cry, but I was already stretching my acting ability to its limits. If I pushed it too far, it'd probably be obvious.

So, I pretended to be a little off balance instead.

Baldrick reached out to steady me.

"Miss Paget," Baldrick said, summoning over the closest servant, "take Miss Grayson to her room. Miss Paget is our newest member, madam. She started this morning, but came with excellent recommendations."

"Okay," I said, not really caring one way or the other.

"The rest of you have duties to perform," Baldrick grumbled, causing the gathered servants to disperse. He then whispered to the young woman who was holding me up. "You take perfect care of the lady, Miss Paget. I don't believe the elderly ladies would have the strength should she become too woozy."

"Yes, Mr. Baldrick," Miss Paget replied smartly.

Miss Paget was definitely *not* a normal. She was easy to read because she kept sniffing the air. It was done almost imperceptibly, and most supernaturals wouldn't have caught on, but I wasn't most supernaturals.

"Let me help you, ma'am," she said, taking my arm and leading me to a large rounded staircase. "I'll get you to your room and then bring you some tea."

I nodded and walked in step with her to the top of the landing.

We turned right and headed down a long hallway that was laced with paintings and gold-etched decor. Obviously, Evelyn Grayson had style *and* money.

My worry was what other things she was involved in.

If this was just a case of inheritance, that would play for a great cover as I spent my nights working for the Black Ops PPD. I still didn't know every facet of what that would entail, but as long as I got the opportunity to assassinate hellions, and I wasn't outed by anyone, I wasn't going to bitch about it.

Too much.

Still, I was seriously out of my element here. Having money was *not* in my bloodline. What *was* in my bloodline was taken by the Houses of Varaz, Mathen, and Tross.

I just needed to survive a year and then they'd pay. One year and I could rule them all, executing each of their reigning members in the process.

Fuckers.

"Ma'am?" Miss Paget said with a grimace as she looked down at her hand.

I released my grip.

"Oh, I'm sorry," I said. "I'm...sorry."

She gave me a slight nod and pushed open the door to my room.

"Get some rest, ma'am," she said, motioning me inside. "I'll bring you tea in a little while." Then she gave me a look and a short nod. *"I'm also available by connector if you need me."*

I jolted slightly, still not used to that whole having people speaking in my head thing.

"Thank you, Miss Paget."

"You can call me Annette through the connector, ma'am."

"Okay," I replied, not looking directly at her. *"Uh...you can call me..."*

Actually, that was a good point. My actual name was Evangeline Sinister, being that we always took our surname as that of the House, but that wasn't exactly a common name. If anyone from the attacking houses heard Evangeline, they'd target in on me instantly.

"What did Evelyn Grayson go by aside from Miss Grayson?"

"Her friends called her 'Eve'."

"Perfect," I said as I entered my room. *"Call me that."*

CHAPTER 14

he room was lavish to the point that it almost made me sick. I would have been able to fit my entire residence in the damn space. Not that I could go back there at the moment.

There were furs and marble and flowers and massive windows and...I didn't even know half the shit I was looking at. I mean, don't get me wrong here, it was magnificent, but members of the Guard weren't entitled to magnificent. It made our asses pucker.

I turned toward a mirror and caught sight of myself. Well, technically I'd caught sight of Evelyn Grayson.

She was decent to look at. Not fae quality, mind you, but who is? She was toned with a pleasing tan, blond hair, and a white bandage on her right cheek.

It was strange to see yourself in a mirror, knowing it wasn't really you. The trick was to pretend you were just at a costume party of sorts.

Even better, don't look at yourself in the mirror.

I sat down at the makeup table that sat in front of the mirror, ignoring my own advice.

Who are you Evelyn Grayson?

Frankly, I couldn't have cared less who she was in the grand scheme of things. My interest was purely a desire of figuring out how I was supposed to act. Was she nice? Mean? Irreverent? I certainly hoped she was irreverent. And she had better have been a damn good drinker, too.

The amnesia trick would hold me over for a while, but eventually she'd...*I'd* get my memories back.

Right?

Just as I crossed my arms and sighed at my new reflection, something brushed across my leg, making me nearly crap myself.

Yes, I was a trained warrior who had seen more battle than most hardened soldiers, but I was completely out of my element here and it was seriously fucking with my head.

I shot a look down at the thing that had caressed my leg.

"Oh, goodie," I said as it jumped onto my lap, obviously not caring one way or the other if I wanted it there, "I have a cat."

After a few moments, and a quick disassociation from my host's heart, I calmed down.

The cat purred as it rubbed against my chest.

I gingerly pet it, though it felt strange to do so. Animals in the Badlands weren't typically friendly. They were there for protection or they were shifters of some sort.

That thought made me give the cat another quick glance.

Nope.

Just a cat. He was black with gray eyes and he had a little white spot on his nose.

It turned and got a look on its face that said it was really interested in jumping over to a cushioned chair by the table where I was seated. I could sense that it was judging the distance. Something told me that it was too far of a jump for the little thing, but I wasn't all that familiar with how dextrous cats were on this plane of existence.

It went for it and missed, bouncing off the side of the chair, but still landing on its feet.

"Shit," it said.

Shit?

How can a cat say 'shit'?

It looked up at me with worry in its eyes.

"Did you just say, 'shit'?" I asked.

"Uh…meow," it replied.

I summoned my blades and had both of them pointing squarely at the cat.

"Shit," it said again.

"Who the fuck are you?" I asked, ready to carve up the little bastard before it had the chance to shift into some other form.

He looked at me, then at my blades, and then back at me again.

"Uh…meow?"

I pressed the point of my right sword against his throat.

"Okay, okay," he said, edging away. "Chill the fuck out." He sat down and peered up at me. "The name is Cruze, and you're clearly *not* Evelyn Grayson. She treats me better and she laughs when I say 'shit'." He scratched at his ear. "To be fair, she's almost *always* drunk. Her and that limo driver of hers..." He glanced up. "Those two fuck like bunnies. Never seen any two people play pokey-pokey like that. That dude has stamina."

"*Had* stamina," I corrected him. "He's dead and so is..." I paused. "*Who* are you, exactly?"

"I told you already," he replied. "My name is Cruze."

"Which tells me nothing other than a name that's most likely made up."

"Aren't *all* names made up?" he countered.

I studied him for a few moments, keeping my blades out just in case.

He looked like a regular cat, at least as far as the ones I'd seen over the years. Small, shifty, and carrying a "what-the-fuck-are-you-staring-at?" look that conveyed precisely where he felt you belonged on the food chain of the relationship.

But there was a problem.

Cats didn't talk.

That meant he was either a shifter or he was being possessed by something. There were only two things that could possess other races: demons and hellions.

"Are you a demon or a hellion?"

His little head jolted slightly, but he quickly recovered and licked his paw.

"I'm a shifter," he answered, "and don't make any short jokes. They're not nice."

"Shift then," I commanded.

"What?"

"Didn't expect me to call your bluff, eh?" I growled, poking him with the blade. "Shift right now, cat, and if you try anything crazy, I'll slice you to bits."

I pulled the sword back slightly to give him room.

He looked up at me for a moment and then closed his eyes.

Nothing happened.

His eyes snapped open again. "Okay, so I'm not a fucking shifter."

"What are you then?" I pressed.

"Not a threat to you, that's what," he shot back.

I pushed the point of the blade at him. He merely stared at me in response.

"Go ahead," he said. "I'm not going to tell you what I am, but I'm also not going to ask precisely what you are either." He tilted his head slightly. "Obviously, like me, you're either a hellion or a demon. I've seen some pretty amazing shifters in my years, but none that can replicate another person so flawlessly, which means you're either possessing Eve or you've killed her and taken over the shell."

"I didn't kill her," I shot back.

"Which affirms that you're not some new brand of shifter," Cruze replied. "That means you're either in hiding or you're up to no good. Whichever really doesn't matter. I won't say anything and neither will you. Win-win, right?"

"Fine," I said, sliding my blades back in their sheaths

and then dismissing them. "I'll let you live for now, but if you double-cross me, I swear that—"

"You'll kill me," Cruze interrupted. "Yeah, yeah, yeah. I get it." He hopped up on to the chair he'd been trying to reach earlier. "If you are hiding, you'd better step up your game at playing the part of Grayson. I was able to trick you into telling me that you weren't a shifter within seconds. That means you're not very good at subterfuge."

I slumped back onto the bench and stared at myself in the mirror.

He was right.

It wasn't like I'd had to spend the majority of my life hiding, though. I was always looking over my shoulder, sure. That's something you learned day one when born into the world of hellions, especially when your mother was a concubine. But I wasn't well-versed in being undercover. If anything, I was raised to hold my head proud and high at being a member of the Guard in the House of Sinister.

"You're not exactly great at it either, you know," I muttered.

"What makes you say that?" Cruze asked, pausing from licking himself.

"A cat who cusses?" I responded, giving him a look.

"Ah, true. I guess I'm just better around people who are drunk."

I leaned back in the chair and stared at him.

At this point, it really didn't matter whether he was a threat to me or not. In his current state, I could kill him in an instant, but I had to sleep sometime. Of course, I could always just throw him out of the room or ask Annette to get rid of him entirely, but something told me that he could prove useful.

I'd have to keep an eye on him, sure, but that was the case with everyone, regardless of whether or not they were 'assigned' to me.

Actually, that was a good point.

"Hey," I said to Cruze, "are you assigned to me, too?"

"Assigned to you?" he asked, his little face contorting slightly. "No, I'm not assigned to you. I thought you were Eve, remember?"

"Yeah, that's true," I sighed. "Sorry. It's been a hell of a day."

He chuckled in a not so funny way. "It's been a hell of a life."

"That, too." I glanced back at the mirror. "I don't suppose you know much about Grayson, do you?"

"Only that she's a ruthless bitch who goes out of her way to crush her enemies at every turn," he answered. "Oh, and that she treats her cat like he's made of gold. Loves me to death. Pets me all the time, gives me the best food a cat could hope for, and even brings over lady cats on a weekly basis so I can get some release."

"You're not *really* a cat, though," I pointed out.

"Yeah," he replied. "It sounded better in my head than it did when it came out. Maybe some hot chicks and a little privacy?"

I ignored that.

Still, he gave me a little information, which was better than nothing. It wasn't much to go on, and I had the feeling that Evelyn Grayson was not as fond of Cruze as he was letting on.

That's when I caught sight of a picture where she was holding the little bugger up close to her, nuzzling against him like he was the greatest thing since perfectly cut diamonds.

Ugh.

"Everyone thinks I have amnesia," I said, after a while. "Selective anyway."

"Don't we all?"

"I mean from the accident."

"What accident?"

"Oh right," I said, "you don't know."

He stopped the licking entirely. "Of course I don't know. I'm a fucking cat. So how about you enlighten me?"

I gave him the lowdown on the accident and how Grayson had died, but I wasn't about to get into how I'd come to be there or why I'd possessed her body.

"You can surmise the rest of what happened," I said to him, keeping the veil of secrecy intact.

"Yeah," the cat replied. "Sucks, though. Eve was a crazy bitch, but she was pretty cool to me. Of course, she didn't know I was anything more than a cat, but still."

I took another glance around the room.

"Anything I should know about this place?" I asked. "Any secrets or hidden rooms?"

He pointed, which looked really weird coming from a cat.

"Over there, behind that wall," he said.

"What's in there?"

"All kinds of crazy shit," he replied. "Whips, chains, and other...stuff."

I cringed.

It was one thing if Evelyn Grayson had been the one delivering punishment, but quite another if she was receiving it. I mean, I enjoyed a rut as much as anyone else, probably more than most, but growing up as the daughter of a concubine taught me that you didn't want to be on the receiving end of the punishment.

"Was she the…uh…" I trailed off.

"She was the top," he answered, giving me a look.

"Good," I said with a gulp. "Still, I won't be playing that game with anyone. I'll just use the amnesia excuse."

"It was only with the limo driver anyway. You're safe."

Whew.

"Point is that it's a hidden room," Cruze continued. "Might be useful in the event a Retriever crew is sent for you."

He was fishing, obviously.

"Nice try," I said with a smirk. "Look, I'm going to get some shut-eye. It's been a hell of a day. If you want to hang out in the whips and chains room while I—"

"I'm good, thanks," he interrupted. "I usually sleep on the bed with you…erm, Eve."

"Yeah, that's about as likely as me dressing up in leather and calling you a bad boy."

"Ew."

CHAPTER 15

The shadows loomed as usual. A brief hum announced each arrival, so that no words were spoken until all were present. It would do no good for any to be overheard when secrecy was paramount.

"We have a use for them?" asked Simone.

"Indeed," replied Leighton. "Willow has shown her hand on the Crest."

A three-dimensional representation of The Crest appeared in the center of the room. It was an area that rested under the city of Los Angeles. There were dungeons and underground dwellings strewn about all of topside, giving supers who had no desire to be found a place to hide out when necessary. The PPD knew about most of them, but not all, and even those they were privy to tended to be off limits to them. This was a matter of practicality. The badge could only protect you so far. But The Crest housed a large shopping center with a nightclub at one end and an adult red-light recreational facility on the other.

A red dot pulsed over the nightclub.

"And you think Willow has the information we need?" Simone asked.

"Obviously," replied Leighton, "or I wouldn't have summoned you."

"I'm talking about the *final* information, Leighton," Simone shot back. "There's no reason to be obstinate."

"I didn't see her," growled Abner, who was supposed to be the watcher of the Crest.

"Making it no less true that she is there," Leighton replied in a haughty tone. "Check the northern tip and you will find a hidden zone has crept in. I have a solid source who tells me she and her crew of bodyguards are in hiding."

Abner said nothing in reply, but it was evident that he was not pleased with having failed to be the first to notice Willow.

"I would happily go and discuss matters with her," suggested Simone. "She listens to me."

Her request was not surprising, seeing that Willow was known to employ only the finest-looking men to act as her bodyguards. They were muscular, handsome, excellent with the blade, and rather adept in the sack. They were also forbidden from wearing shirts.

"That will not be necessary," Leighton stated as Abner grunted yet again. "We need answers from Willow sooner rather than later, and I believe we all remember what happened the last time you encountered Willow's guards."

"*I* most certainly do," Simone breathed.

There was a moment of silence.

"Precisely," continued Leighton, "which is why we'll go about utilizing our professionals this time around."

CHAPTER 16

I woke up to a ringing sound in my head. It wasn't like a cell phone or an alarm clock. I'd have to say that it sounded like a servant's bell. A ting-a-ling sort of thing that just rang of superiority.

I felt as though I was in the middle of the worst hangover I'd ever had. The events of the previous day had bent my brain pretty badly, and the memory of watching Garrick fall was enough to put me in a full state of despair. Losing House Sinister was no picnic either, of course, but not so much because of the people who lived there. It was more a case of it being my charge to defend it, and I'd been unable to do my fair share.

Were Garrick standing here, he would have claimed that I was doing more to save the House now than any amount of swordplay would have allowed.

And he would have been right.

Still, something deep inside me burned to have fallen by the blade instead of running from it.

Ting-a-ling-a-ling.

I grunted and opened my eyes.

That's when I saw the body of a cat lying next to me.

He was on his back with his lower legs splayed out, and his mouth was slightly open. I would have thought he'd been shot were it not for the wiggling of his eyes beneath their lids coupled with the rhythmic sound of snoring. I'd never had a pet before, and knowing that there was either a demon or a hellion living inside this little feline, I was quite aware that I did *not* have one now.

With a sigh, I pulled up the blanket and gently covered him.

"Fucking cat," I whispered with a grin.

Ting-a-ling-a-ling.

"Oh, for fuck's sake," I grumbled, sliding carefully out of bed and stepping down the stairs that led to the little table I'd been seated at the night before. "What?"

Ting-a-ling-a-ling.

"What?" I asked again.

Clearly, I was doing something wrong, as there was no response. The ringing was definitely coming through my head, through the connector thing that had been installed into my brain.

I focused on it until it rang again, and then I mentally 'pushed' a button, forcing myself to *think* my words.

"*Hello?*"

"*It's about time,*" came the voice of Q. "*You are required at the main headquarters. We are awaiting your arrival.*"

"*Okay,*" I replied. "*Any suggestions on how exactly I should get there?*"

"*Your tattoo.*"

I glanced down at my left forearm and looked over the black lines.

It wasn't technically a tattoo, at least not in the traditional sense. I hadn't sat down at a parlor as an artist used a machine to manually draw on my flesh, anyway. Supposedly, there was a machine option that was lorded over by a goblin in Netherworld Proper for PPD officers to get their initiate tats. I'd seen that on a training video in the Guard that was intended on teaching us how to deal with cops in the event that we ran into them. It had been a very short video.

My tattoo was drawn by nanites, and they'd done it from the inside, connecting it through my body somehow.

There was a single line running from my wrist about two inches up. From there, it split into a mirrored design that was full of sharp points and rounded angles. It was fractal in nature and it ended in a long point from a disassociated piece on the opposite side.

"*Right, my tattoo,*" I said, finally. "*So what exactly am I supposed to do with this?*"

"*You didn't read the manual?*" Q nearly shrieked.

I scrunched my brow. "*What manual?*"

"*The one...*" He trailed off. "*Let me guess: Kayson did not provide you with the manual, right?*"

"*Ding ding ding,*" I blurted. "*What do we have for him, Johnny?*" There was no response. "*Sorry. No, I didn't get a manual.*"

"*Ridiculous,*" he hissed. "*It's not like the man has many jobs. All he does is eat, sleep, kill, and have sexual relations with most anything that has an available orifice.*"

Speaking of available orifices. The image of Kayson filled my head, reminding me of how attractive he was. Plus, the knowledge of the fact that he was a hellwolf was pretty intoxicating. Not if he was in wolf mode, obviously, but his human look was quite attractive.

"I know that look," Cruze announced as he climbed down the stairs. "Eve used to get it all the time." He motioned toward the hidden area with the whips and chains. "That's why she built the room."

I shook myself back to reality.

Great, so Eve's sexual nature was somehow mixing with my own libido, which was already high enough as it was. The combination of the two was proving to be pretty intense.

I'd have to keep myself in check.

"*Anyway,*" Q instructed, "*place the middle finger of your right hand at the tip of the tattoo near your wrist. Put your thumb on the tip near the inside of your elbow. Slide your fingers toward each other until the lines split. Remove your fingers and press the center design for three seconds.*"

"Then, what?"

"*Then, you'll be here,*" he answered.

"*Okay, but I was told not to portal from here.*"

"*By whom?*"

"My limo driver," I answered. "*She said it wasn't safe.*"

He sighed. "*That's probably true. Okay, well, get here as soon as you can. The Directors aren't the kind who enjoy being left waiting.*"

He disconnected before I could reply.

I walked to the bathroom to clean myself up. There

was a toothbrush hanging there, but it felt kind of gross to use it, even if it *did* belong to the body I was inhabiting.

"How do I get one of the butlers or whatever up here?"

Cruze actually managed to raise an eyebrow.

"Uh," he said, "you *don't* have that kind of relationship with any of them. Well, except the limo driver, but you said that he was—"

"I'm not looking to get laid, cat," I interrupted, though I warmed slightly at the thought. "I want someone to buy me some fresh supplies."

"Why?"

"Because…" I stopped and gave him a look. "Because I want them, that's why."

"Okay, okay," he said, sitting back and putting up his paws in surrender. "You don't have to be a bitch about it." Then he tilted his head. "Hey, wait. Are you having PMS or something?"

I closed my eyes and took a deep breath.

"Unless you want to be neutered this afternoon, I would—"

"Too late," he grunted. "This cat was already snipped before I jumped in."

"Fine," I stated in a cold voice. "Unless you want me to sew on a fresh set of balls and *then* cut them back off, I'd suggest you tell me how to get some fucking help around here."

His eyes went incredibly wide as he pointed and rasped, "Blue button…by the door."

CHAPTER 17

*M*iss Paget, or Annette, as she preferred to be called in private, had hooked me up with fresh supplies and helped me select an outfit that Evelyn Grayson would normally wear.

It was a simple blouse and slacks combination that fit perfectly, accentuating Evelyn's parts just right. The shoes were both comfortable and strange. I wasn't one who was used to wearing heels, unless they were thick and wide and attached to boots. A stiletto was something entirely different in my world. The heals I'd worn home from the hospital were very short, so I hadn't struggled much with those, but these were a bit taller and thinner.

"I don't know about this," I said to Annette. "I feel like a baby deer in these things."

"You'll get used to it," she replied. "Remember, it's important that you maintain the proper look."

"Which I will fail at miserably if I end up twisting my ankle because I'm incapable of walking around in heels."

"Fair enough," she agreed before setting out to find

something a little less of a challenge. "We are going to have to practice, though. Jimmy Choo, Miu Miu, Manolo Blahnik, and Louis Vuitton make up the majority of this closet."

I peered inside and only saw shoes. "Sorry, who?"

"My point is that you can't walk around in flats all the time. Miss Grayson was known for her heels."

Another glance at the sex room told me she was known for more than just heels. Though, to be fair, a number of her shoes looked like they fit the part of a woman who enjoyed carrying a whip.

I was fine playing the part of Evelyn Grayson to a point, but I *did* have my limitations.

"The House is the priority…always," came the words of Garrick from deep in my mind.

"Yeah, okay," I said, finally, "I'll practice walking on the damn things *and* using a whip."

She frowned at me. "A whip?"

"Never mind that," I replied quickly. "Let's just get me into some shoes that will work for now. I have to get to a meeting with the Directors."

I slipped on a pair of black pumps and then headed out the door and down the stairs.

Baldrick bowed his "Good morning" to me and led me into the dining room. There was a plate with scrambled eggs and fruit. I was more of a biscuits and gravy type, or at least sausage and bacon, but I couldn't really say anything just yet. I'd have to work that into the overall conversation of what Evelyn Grayson was going to become. Using amnesia as an excuse was ideal in that it would allow me to mix my own personality in and start running things my way. Given a few months, nobody would even notice the changes. As long as it wasn't abrupt, it would work.

I hoped.

Based on what I'd seen of Grayson, I was actually more empathetic anyway. Now, that may not seem like something you'd expect to hear from a hellion, but you have to remember that I wasn't someone who grew up with a silver spoon in my mouth. Hell, if it hadn't been for my killing of a man, and Garrick's subsequent intervention, I'd likely be spending these years of my life with something entirely different in my mouth.

That was a disturbing thought, but it was one that kept me pushing to be my best.

I never blamed my mother for what she had to resort to doing in order to feed and clothe me, but I *did* swear that I would never do the same. And I would do my damndest to help other people out of that life every chance I had.

With the money afforded me here, under the name of Evelyn Grayson, there was a strong possibility that I could accomplish that, but only if I was cunning in how I changed the narrative.

After downing my food, I rose and walked toward the main door.

"Miss Paget informed me that you wish to visit the office today, Madam," Baldrick said as he stepped to the door. "Do you feel healthy enough for such an endeavor?"

Based on his expression, I had the feeling that the real Evelyn would have chastised him and said a few choice words to ensure he'd be put directly back in his place.

Again, it was time to change the narrative.

"I appreciate the concern, Baldrick," I said, carrying only a slight edge to my voice. "I'll be fine. If anything happens, I'll simply have the driver return me home."

"As you wish, Madam," Baldrick replied with a slight nod as he opened the door.

I stepped through to find Rainey was already waiting for me beside a deep purple vehicle that looked rather expensive.

She opened the door and I got inside, finding myself seated in a white leather seat with purple accents. There were little dots of lights on the ceiling and a tray stuck out from the seat in front of me. On it was a small screen.

Rainey closed me in and then walked around to take the driver's seat.

Once she drove away, she glanced at the rearview mirror.

"Did you get any rest?"

"Some," I answered, still in awe of the fancy vehicle I was riding in. "What is this car?"

"Pretty sweet, right?" she said, all smiles. "It's called a Rolls Royce Phantom. Drives like a dream."

And it rode like one, too.

The limousine Rainey had taken me home in was nice, but I'd been in a limo before. Once a year, members of the Guard were given a party in their honor. Fine food, a nice show, and elegant transportation. You didn't get to go every year because duty came first, and not all members of the Guard could be traipsing about drunk and full of food, but the couple of times I was selected to attend were impressive.

This felt different, though. It was somehow nicer than a limo. It wasn't as large, no, but that only added to its allure. To me, anyway. It felt like anyone could rent a limousine, but to have one of these fancy vehicles seemed like a level of posh I wasn't used to seeing, and I definitely had never experienced it.

"So where are we going?" asked Rainey, jolting me from my shock and awe. "Maybe hit the mall and do a little shopping? You have tons of money."

"Ah, no," I replied. "I have to get to a meeting with the Directors."

"Oh!" Her playful attitude instantly changed over. "If it's urgent, you can just go ahead and portal out from here. I can drive downtown and mill around for a while, pretending that you are just looking at the various sites."

"Wouldn't that look suspicious?"

"The windows are blackened," she answered. "Nobody can see you. Plus, people tend not to bother Miss Grayson. She has…had a bit of a reputation."

I nodded.

"What other options are there?" I asked. "I understand that she…*I* have an office somewhere?"

"Downtown, yes," Rainey replied. "I can take you there, if you'd prefer?"

"Yeah, do that. I don't want anything to look suspect."

Rainey nodded and moved to a different lane.

I had no idea where I was, other than Los Angeles, so I could only assume that she knew where she was going.

"Were you able to learn anything new that might help me play the part of Grayson?" I asked, after a few turns. "I'm still planning to keep with the amnesia angle, but I'll take whatever I can get about her life and personality. I'm not a fan of being blindsided."

"Not a lot," she replied, sounding unhappy with herself. "You run a number of non-profit organizations, all from the building I'm taking you to. You're also the heir to tons of real estate, all of which was left to you by your father, who was quite a mogul."

"Hotels or something?"

"Land," she answered. "There are many pieces with hotels built on them, but you own the land."

I was never one to spend my time prospecting real estate. That wasn't the life of a Guard. However, I had heard a number of conversations over my years on protection duty to know that land was the most important asset of all. The buildings were nice, but location was paramount.

"Okay, so I own a lot of land," I mused. "Do I have to do anything with it?"

"No. It's all taken care of by employees. You *do* have regular meetings with a board of directors, but that's not for another couple of weeks. Hopefully, by then, we'll have more information for you to use as you morph into the role of Evelyn Grayson."

"Yeah, I'm not doing that," I stated, looking out the window.

"What?"

"I'm going to play up the amnesia bit for quite a while," I explained. "I'll have flashes of memories come back, but if the body I'm in housed the mind of a serious bitch, that's going to change some. People will buy it because of the horrific accident I was in. Getting knocked in the head does things to people."

The car grew quiet for a few minutes as we continued toward the office that I'd apparently owned...or rented... or whatever they did up here. Rainey'd said that I only owned land, so I assumed that the building was just a rental. Hell, maybe I only had a small office there?

"I'm sorry, but do you really think that's wise?" Rainey ventured, breaking the silence. "I mean, there's some reason you're hiding in that body in the first place. Now, I don't have all the details, but I know how it works in our community. You're either a demon or a hellion. My guess is the latter, due to the news that is coming up from the Badlands, but I seriously don't want to dig any further than that. Regardless, my point is that you're hiding from something. The more you act like Grayson, the less people will notice anything out of the ordinary. If you start tweaking her personality, though, that's going to raise some flags...especially if you really screw with things."

She was right, of course, and I would be cautious in how I played things, but I wasn't just going to be a bitch for the sake of being a bitch. From what I'd been told by the few people who knew Grayson, she was a bitch. That may not have been her public persona, but she clearly came across that way in one-on-one situations. Baldrick's look at the door was indicative of that, not to mention all those gadgets in the sex room.

"I'll be careful," I assured Rainey, though I didn't know why I felt the need. It wasn't like she was my boss or anything. She could have been playing the role of informant, of course, but even then she wouldn't want to provide too much information to her superiors. If they felt she couldn't control me, she'd be replaced. With the knowledge she housed, being replaced wouldn't likely result in a simple job reassignment. "My plan is to just tweak the edges a little bit. Nothing drastic."

Maybe.

CHAPTER 18

The office was as posh as the Rolls Royce, at least from the outside. Glass windows that held a blue tint sat alongside perfectly-cleaned white concrete. There were palm trees around it as well. It was…idyllic.

We drove into a parking area that led downward. When we reached the bottom of the ramp, I spotted a few other vehicles that looked as fancy as mine. None of them were limousines, either. Of course, the likelihood of a limo fitting in this special garage was unlikely.

"Where are we, exactly?"

"It's just the personal garage of the wealthier business owners in the building," Rainey replied. She parked and got out, coming around to open the door for me. "The elevator over there will take your handprint and bring you directly to your suite."

"You're not coming with me?" I asked as I stepped out of the car.

She gave me a funny look. "I think that'd look kind of strange, wouldn't you?"

"Why?"

"You don't think that having your chauffeur walk around the office with you is odd?"

I closed my eyes for a second. "True. It would be. Sorry, I'm just…"

I sighed.

"You're lost and out of your element," she said, her eye roving around the area. "I get it, but this is where I have to stay. I can tell you that you'll be faced with a receptionist when you get up there. Just ask them where your office is and let them feel sorry for you."

"Yeah," I said, finding it funny that I felt more nervous about this than I did about facing three soldiers with sharpened weapons. "I'll handle it."

I started walking toward the elevator, but stopped and turned back.

"Thanks for all the help, Rainey," I said. "I appreciate it."

"You're welcome," she replied with a smile. "But, listen, the real Grayson wouldn't have just said that. In fact, she wouldn't have given two shits about me."

I smiled back and then spun to put my hand on the reader at the elevator.

The doors opened, revealing an opulent lift that was covered in marble and gold etchings. I walked in and the doors closed. There were no buttons or anything. It just started moving until my ears popped. Then it slowed and the doors opened again.

Just as Rainey had said, there was a large reception

desk with a classily-etched sign that read Grayson Holdings, Ltd.

The woman smiled brightly at me. There was a hint of something behind those sparkling eyes that appeared less than friendly, though. Just another indicator that Evelyn wasn't exactly liked.

How could a person go through their entire life like that? I'd had a tougher life than most and even I had friends and did my best to treat people with respect… those who deserved it, at least.

"Miss Grayson," she said in a voice that was almost too eager, "it is wonderful to see you back so soon."

Somehow, I doubted that.

"Thank you," I replied, smiling back. That obviously caught her off guard, but I quickly rolled with it. "I have lost a fair deal of my memory, so you'll please forgive that I don't remember your name."

She blinked a few times. "Truly?"

"I am sorry."

"No, no," she said, stepping around the large desk and approaching me. "I'm not worried about the fact that you've not remembered my name. I'm more concerned that you're suffering amnesia."

"It's rather trying, I must say."

I don't know why I had the desire to speak more eloquently around these people. It felt like the right thing to do, though. I'm not saying I was going out of my way to look for grand words or deep sentences, but I *did* find myself wanting to say "yes" instead of "yeah." I didn't feel the same around Rainey or Annette, but I guess that's because they knew what was really going on…or some version of it, anyway.

"If you could point me toward my office, please?" I asked, not quite wanting the already awkward situation to turn into a hug and a pat on the back. "I'm hoping that being in there for a little while may jog a memory or two."

"Of course," she replied, almost chipper. "Follow me."

We walked to the right of the reception desk and down through a small corridor. It opened into a larger room that was filled with workers, each in a cubicle. While there was separation, the walls were glass. This would give them some semblance of sound-deadening, but it wouldn't let them have visual privacy.

As I walked by, faces turned to glance in my direction.

Their faces were the same as how the receptionist's had been.

Fake.

They weren't happy to see Evelyn Grayson in the least. They were playing a game that made them appear as though they were glad to see her, but each set of eyes told me that they held some level of disappointment that Grayson had survived the accident.

All the more reason to make minor shifts in my personality.

The receptionist stopped at the foot of a set of stairs that led up to an office. It had a large glass window that overlooked the pit of workers.

Evil.

"I'm sorry," I said to the woman, "but what is your name again?"

"Maria, ma'am."

"Just call me Eve, please," I replied. She blinked at me. I leaned in, feigning concern. "Is that not okay?"

"Uh…no, no, it's fine," she replied. "It's just that you are usually very formal with your employees, ma'am…Eve."

"I see," I said, studying the faces in the room.

After a small smile, I climbed the stairs and turned around to face them all.

"Everyone," I said, feeling somewhat nervous, "I'm sure you all have heard that I was in an automobile accident." Their heads nodded. "Apparently, I'm going to be fine, but I have suffered some effects of amnesia. I remember certain things, but not others. For example, I don't know any of your names, except for Maria here now, but that's only because I've just asked."

Everyone smiled at that.

Those were genuine.

"Maria tells me that I was pretty formal before, so I'll understand if you want to maintain that formality." I took in a deep breath. "I wouldn't want anyone to feel as if I would suddenly regain my memories and then feel an urge of angst at you for being informal."

I cleared my throat.

"Look," I added, trying to show my frustration, "I don't really know who I was or how I acted. Based on the responses I've had from a number of people, I can't help but imagine that I was kind of a bi…" I paused. "That I was somewhat difficult."

They were exchanging glances at this point.

"Based on your reaction to my admission, I can see that was indeed the case." I ran my hand through my hair. "Okay, well, in the event that I may never fully regain my memories, which I was told is a very real possibility, I'm going to go with the less informal route. Again, there is no requirement from your side to do the same, and if you would prefer that I use your formal name, that's perfectly fine." I glanced around once more. "I'm going to offer up that you just call me Eve, though."

You could have heard a pin drop.

"Well, all that said," I chuckled, trying to further show that the new Eve was human, "I'm going to go into my office for a little while and try and jog my memories. If I could have a few hours of privacy, I would appreciate it."

They all nodded.

One hand went up. It belonged to a young man who had dark brown hair and deep blue eyes. Something told me I knew him…in the Biblical sense…more than once.

"Yes?" I asked.

"If you press the red button on the inside of your desk, your windows will darken and you'll have complete privacy."

"Thank you," I said as I turned and entered my office.

When I got to the other side of my desk, I looked back out and saw all their faces were still on me. One by one, they turned back to their work, looking like they'd just been caught going through their father's porn stash.

Well, if nothing else, I'd started down the path of tweaking the personality of Evelyn Grayson. I'd have to show some level of bitch at some point, but for now I was going to keep playing it cool.

I pressed the red button and saw that all of the windows had indeed darkened, including the ones that allowed me to look out at the skyline. The door also locked.

"*I'm assuming you'll be heading to meet with the Directors?*" asked a voice that was clearly the same man who told me to use the red button.

"*Yes,*" I replied, cautiously. "*What is your name?*"

"*Julian. There are a few of us on the team who are aware of the situation. We don't know the details, for obvious reasons, but we know enough. We'll make sure nobody bothers you until you return.*"

"*Thank you, Julian,*" I said, but then stopped for a second. "*Were you all working here before?*"

"*Yes, why?*"

"*Exactly my question. Why were you working here before?*"

"*Uh...*" he started and then stopped. "*I mean, it pays well, we get to help a lot of people, and, frankly, Miss Grayson was really good in the sack.*"

Nice.

"*So this was just a normal...*mostly *normal job for you all, then?*"

"*Up until now, yes,*" he answered. "*However, if you want to continue the tryst that I had going on with Miss Grayson, I'm game.*"

He *was* good-looking, and I *was* hornier than usual, but something told me not to make any commitments just yet.

"*I'll keep you posted on that,*" I told him.

"*Good enough for me.*"

At that, I pulled up my sleeve and followed the instructions Q had given me to transport to headquarters.

CHAPTER 19

You will always learn more when no answer is given to
the most pertinent of questions.

— GARRICK - HOUSE OF SINISTER

"*I*t's about time you arrived," Quinton said,
glaring at me as he led me into a room that
looked very familiar. "I'll let them know we're all *finally*
here."

I'm not sure what I was expecting, but I certainly
hadn't thought I'd be entering a brightly-lit room with
theater seating. There was a screen at the front of the
room and everything.

It was currently blank.

I'd felt like I'd gone to the movies and was waiting for
the lights to go down.

Popcorn would have been nice.

Q took a seat at a little table between the theater seats
and the screen.

Kayson was to my left, leaning back with his hands behind his head and his feet up.

"They recline?" I asked as I sat next to him, instantly realizing that it was a stupid question.

"Button on the inside of the right arm," he replied, thankfully not giving me any grief. "Don't drop it back too far, though." He opened one eye and peered at me. "I won't be responsible if you start snoring when we're talking to the brass."

I gave him a half-smile in response.

"They'll be here any moment," Q announced over his shoulder. "I would appreciate it if you would demonstrate a little professionalism for once, Kayson."

"Nah, I'm good."

Q took a deep breath and let it go as my finger hovered over the button that reclined the chair.

I felt as though I were at a bit of a crossroads right then. On the one hand, I could lean the chair back and set the tone of who I was straight out of the gate; on the other hand, I could be a little more formal, possibly even taking one of the wooden chairs at the table next to Q, thereby providing a more professional attitude to my new bosses. The thing was that I didn't know if they were more like Q or Kayson.

Maybe they preferred the laid back assassin to the anal retentive?

Finally, I decided that the best course of action was to go neutral. I stayed in the nice leather chair, but kept it in the upright position.

"What exactly—"

"Shhh," snapped Q, barely looking back. "They'll be here momentarily."

I wasn't used to being spoken to like that, and I certainly had no plans to tolerate it. Before I'd had the chance to educate the vampire, though, the lighting dimmed slightly.

Q stood up respectfully until three dark boxes appeared, floating in the air roughly five feet away from the movie screen. They were equidistant from each other about halfway up to the ceiling.

Part of me wanted to stand as well, but the evident fear flowing through Q was enough to make me question whether or not these Directors deserved my respect. I'd been taught to give the benefit of the doubt to people I'd never met before. Garrick drilled that into our heads during training, and specifically singled me out because of my legacy, but even then I knew when to be polite and when to hold steady.

"Quinton," said a deep voice that emanated from the center box, "I trust all is well?"

"Yes, Director Leighton," he replied in a formal tone. "We have brought the new recruit with us." He turned to me. "Stand up!"

I gave him a dark look before finally getting to my feet.

"I don't believe she appreciates your demanding attitude, Quinton," laughed the voice of a woman who was part of the right box. "You may wish to control yourself around her."

Q glared at me.

"You might want to listen to the right box, Q," I agreed.

"I know I'm the new kid on the block here, but I'm not used to being bossed around by lesser races."

"Lesser races?" Q blurted. "You consider a vampire as less than a hellion?"

"Who doesn't?" I replied.

Kayson laughed, throwing a thumbs-up while keeping his eyes closed.

"Yeah," he said, "she's going to work out just fine on this team."

"Nobody asked you, Kayson," snapped Q.

"Enough," Leighton stated, quieting us as a parent would children. "I am Leighton. The female you heard speaking is Simone. On my other side is Abner. We are the Directors of this group."

"And this is the Black Ops section of the Paranormal Police Department," I finished for him. "Q and Kayson already filled me in on the basics. I just don't know the specifics. Frankly, I don't even know if I want to be involved at all. Assassinations are fine with me, especially if I get to wipe out other hellions—and dragons, too—but running around killing people I don't know just doesn't seem all that honorable."

"If we tell you to kill someone, you will do so without hesitation," Leighton replied. "Your honor is not a concern of ours, I'm afraid."

Well, that answered my question over whether or not they deserved my respect.

"I don't give a shit if it concerns you or not," I countered. "It *is* a concern of mine."

There was a moment of silence.

"Quinton," Simone said, "take Kayson and leave the room, please. We will speak with Evangeline directly."

"Yes, ma'am," Q said, rushing off and shoving at Kayson's legs. "Come on, Kayson. You heard her."

"Yeah, yeah, yeah," Kayson said as his chair slowly righted itself. "Keep smacking my legs, Q, and I'll kick your ass."

Q grunted and strode from the room.

"Have fun," Kayson added to me before he followed after Q.

As soon as the doors shut, I turned back toward the three boxes and crossed my arms. I had no idea what to expect, but I had the feeling they knew more about me than they'd told Kayson and Q. That didn't mean I was just going to roll over and bare my stomach to them, though. Sure, I might put up a front, but then I'd get the hell out and find a new place to hide.

"Have a seat," suggested Leighton.

"I'll stand," I replied.

A few seconds went by, telling me that Leighton was not one who was used to having his orders disobeyed. I was fine with that, seeing as I wasn't used to being the only remaining person of a House who was being hunted like a rabid animal.

"As you wish," he said, finally. "The fact of the matter is that we know who you are, why you're topside, and what will happen to you if your true identity is discovered."

My blood went cold.

Simone spoke next. "We're also more than capable of sending information to the Houses of Varaz, Mathen, and Tross in order to pinpoint your precise whereabouts, including the details regarding the body you're currently inhabiting."

The proverbial barrel stood before me, waiting for me to bend over it.

"The story we'll tell," added Abner, from the box on the left, "is that you possessed the form of Evelyn Grayson before she died."

My eyes went wide. "I did no such thing."

"Your word against ours," Leighton countered. "Who do you think the hellions will believe? Those who hold the highest positions in all topside or the word of a concubine's daughter?"

"Fuck you," I shot back, stepping toward the box.

A red beam of light shot out from it instantly, striking my thigh and dropping me to the ground. The pain was intense, causing every muscle in my body to cramp. It was so horrible that I couldn't even make a sound, until the beam ceased.

I groaned while trying to catch my breath.

"It is suggested that you not try to attack us, Evangeline," Simone snarked. "You may be used to many things in your little world, but you've just entered an arena that is far more powerful than you can even imagine."

The pain was slowly subsiding, but I continued to lie on my back and catch my breath.

"If that's so," I rasped, "why do you need me at all?"

"To cover our tracks," answered Abner.

"Correct," agreed Leighton. "Just because we are of the true ruling class doesn't mean we're foolish, and even though all members at our level partake in their own forms of…let's call it 'life management,' none of us wish to have our names directly tied to even the most necessary of atrocities."

Translation: It wasn't any different than what I'd already dealt with as a Guard of House Sinister. Maybe it was on a larger scale, but it was just the same shit on a different day.

Not that they would admit to that. Nor would they likely provide me any depth of what their actual purposes were, but it was worth a shot.

"So, you're the ruling class?" I asked.

There was no answer.

"That implies that there is nobody above you on the food chain," I continued. "Yet, at the same time, you worry about having your names tied to anything that we, your Black Ops crew, does. Curious."

Their silence continued.

Garrick was right. I learned more about these three from their lack of answers than I would have from anything they could have made up. They were cowards, hiding behind their riches, pulling strings for their own amusement. Again, it was precisely like the high elders back in the Houses.

That's when a thought struck me. "Am I even truly an officer of the law? I mean, I'm not exactly what you would consider pure of spirit…or mind." I snorted at myself. "And definitely *not* of body."

"What does purity have to do with anything?" asked Abner.

By now I was feeling well enough to push myself up to a seated position, hugging my knees against my chest.

"I'm just saying that it's more likely that I would break the law than uphold it," I answered. "Then again, the very fact that I'll be performing assassinations pretty much knocks that whole 'upholding the law' thing on its ass."

"Now you're understanding things," Leighton replied.

"Almost," stated Abner. "It should be noted that those you will be assassinating are beyond reproach."

"Most of them, anyway," agreed Simone. "And also bear in mind that you won't *only* be performing assassinations. There are many types of missions you'll be sent on."

I nodded and got back to my feet, moving slowly backward to avoid another shot in the leg.

Everything was happening very fast. I escaped a dying House, inhabited the body of a dead woman, got inducted into Black Ops, was given a tattoo and a connector, learned that I had a cat, and was now being told that I was a cop.

Or was I?

"So," I ventured, "am I a cop or not?"

"Technically, you *are* an officer of the Paranormal Police Department," answered Leighton. "At the same time, you are above their general jurisdiction, including even the Retrievers and the Executive Directors. Aside from us, you answer to no one."

That was both good and bad. It was good because it meant that I knew where my chain of command was, and that gave me a leash just long enough to hang myself. It was bad because I wasn't exactly what you might call 'police material.' If anything, I was more built to be a part of the criminal element.

The truth was that it seemed like Black Ops was just a somewhat lawful way to employ incredibly effective criminals, so maybe it was actually a win-win.

Either way, this little conversation made it clear that I was equally as dead here if I fucked up as I would be if Moloch and his goons found me.

"So, Evangeline," Leighton asked in an amused voice, "do you wish us to notify the Houses of your whereabouts or are you ready to accept your position in Black Ops?"

"I'll accept the position," I answered, "but only if it's understood that I will never back away from the opportunity to kill anyone from Varaz, Mathen, and Tross."

"As long as it doesn't interfere with our needs," stated Leighton. "Otherwise, it will be forbidden."

Well, if that time ever came, I'd find myself asking for forgiveness instead of permission.

"Now," Leighton said quickly, "let's discuss your first mission."

CHAPTER 20

I walked out of the room with the details on the mission. The Directors wanted us to pull information from a contact by the name of Willow. They didn't care *how* we got the information, as long as we got it.

Kayson and Q were waiting in the lobby. Turned out that it *was* a movie theater. Kayson was finishing up a hotdog and a stupidly large drink.

"Looks healthy," I said as Q rushed up to me.

"What did they say?" the vampire nearly pleaded. "Anything about me?"

Without hesitation, I snapped a perfectly aimed fist at the center of his face, sending him flying backwards over a fake plant. He crashed to the ground with a groan.

"Boss me around again, asshole," I warned him as I stepped over and dropped to stick my knee on his throat, "and you'll pray to have a wooden stake driven through your heart."

"Tee-hee-hee," giggled Kayson. That was followed by

the slurping sound of a drink that had only shards of ice remaining. "Nice punch."

I pushed away from Q, gave him a final glare to drive home my point, and then began walking toward the main door. It wasn't like I knew where I was going, but I at least needed to make a show of it. The last thing I wanted was for some worthless vampire to think he had the upper hand in this relationship. A hellwolf having the upper hand was acceptable, if only for a night, but I knew when and where to express my dominance, and this was it.

"We've been tasked with extracting information from someone named Willow," I said as I strode purposefully toward the door.

"And you think she's in the parking lot?" Kayson called out.

I stopped.

"Does this mean you know where she is?" I asked.

"No," he answered after a long slurp from the ice at the bottom of the proverbial bucket he was drinking from, "but I'm guessing she's not out there." He then furrowed his brow. "Then again, maybe? I don't know. We've never gone out that way before."

Shit.

"Fine," I grumbled. "Where do we find her, then?"

"Fuck if I know," Kayson answered with a shrug. "That's Q's gig."

I tilted my head towards Q. He was back up on his feet and rubbing his neck.

"Do you know where Willow is?"

"Not off the top of my head, no," he answered angrily,

"but it's my job to lay out the plan and set everything up to ensure the fewest casualties possible."

"Oh," I replied, suddenly feeling as though I may have jumped the gun on things. "So, you're not an assassin?"

Kayson belted out a laugh. "He's a fucking accountant, and not even a good one."

"Pardon me?"

"Why are you a part of Black Ops again?" asked Kayson quickly, sounding like he was turning a few screws in the process. "Got caught with your hands in the cookie jar, right? Idiot."

"Like you're any better," Q shot back.

"Nope, but I don't try to be. I know what I am, and I'm totally cool with that."

He jumped up from his chair and threw away his trash.

"Here's the deal," Kayson explained as he wiped his hands on his pants, "you and me are the muscle and Q is the brains. I know that's a scary proposition," he added with a face of mock concern, "but the fact is that he sucks at killing—well, fighting in general, actually—and I don't like planning shit. So, unless you *do* like planning shit, it's best to just let him figure out all the technicalities while we lounge around not doing much. Once he's figured out where our target is, we put on our gear and go kill shit."

With that, he leaped over the counter and reached inside to grab a box of Snowcaps.

"Want some?"

"No, thanks," I replied, feeling confused by his cavalier attitude, but something about it was comforting.

"Anyway," he continued while tearing open the box, "any questions?"

It was pretty straightforward. Q was in charge of making sure we knew precisely where we were going and what we were doing before we ever stepped out and started taking people down. That meant that Q had contacts, or at least skills and data that I certainly did *not* have topside. At least, not yet.

But there was one thing that troubled me.

"What gear?"

"Huh?" asked Kayson.

"You said we had to put on our gear," I reminded him.

"Oh, well, you're not going to wear *that*, right?"

I looked down at myself, recalling that I had on a nice blouse with dark pants. It wasn't really my kind of garb, but it was something Evelyn Grayson wore in many of the pictures that adorned her room, and Annette felt it represented my host-body's look best.

"No good?" I asked, feeling unsure.

"It's okay if you're going to an interview," Kayson replied with a shrug. Then, he looked up at me. "Ah. Right. I guess you kind of just did, huh?"

"A little bit, yeah."

He nodded and then threw the empty box into the trash.

"Come on, Q," he said as he walked over and patted the vampire on the shoulder. "Let's head back down to the office so you can get to work on finding Willow and I can help Eve get out of her clothes."

I cracked a smile at his phrasing while following them down a flight of stairs.

At the bottom of the second level, they walked directly through a wall. I'd sensed the null zone, but the fact that they had disappeared before my eyes told me there was also a hidden zone there.

Kayson stepped back through a moment later.

"Sorry," he said. "The exit sign right there is the indicator for where to walk. Just step through and—"

"I know what a hidden zone is," I interrupted, walking past him and directly into a half-opened door that was on the other side. "Ouch."

"Sorry," Kayson said. "The, uh, door was still open."

I rubbed my nose and gave him a look.

"Right. Well, follow me."

We walked into a relatively small office that had a few desks. It was clean and sterile, much like I'd assumed Q's house would have been decorated. I would have preferred something darker, personally.

I shook my head. "So our base of operations is inside of an actual movie theater?"

"What gave it away?" asked Q snidely.

"I was being rhetorical," I replied, but then let my guard down a bit. "Listen, I'm sorry I punched you in the face."

"Why are you apologizing to him?" Kayson asked, almost looking injured himself. "You were doing so well up until then."

"Shut up, Kayson," Q grunted, before turning back to me. "You were saying?"

I opened and closed my mouth a few times while squinting at Kayson.

Finally, I looked back at Q and said, "I'm sorry, is all.

But if you think you're going to boss me around, you're dead wrong. Keep it up and I'll keep punching you."

"Redeemed," Kayson announced with a shit-eating grin. "Now that we've got that all taken care of, how about we get you outfitted?"

With that, he turned and headed toward the back of the office.

"Should I be worried?" I asked Q before heading after Kayson.

"With him around," Q replied, turning his attention to his desk, "I'm *always* worried."

CHAPTER 21

Use every advantage, no matter how insignificant it may seem.

— GARRICK - HOUSE OF SINISTER

I understood the importance of wearing the proper garb when doing a job. While I was in this business outfit for my interview, donning it for an assassination attempt would probably not be the best choice. That had nothing to do with the fact that it was a nice shirt that wouldn't look all that great with blood on it, but rather that I would stand out like a beacon if I wore it walking into a den of thieves.

That wasn't necessarily a bad thing.

It *would* throw them off their guard a bit. But it would only do so once. After that, word would flow through the criminal element pipeline that there was an assassin walking around in business attire.

Eventually, my face would be recognized anyway, but that would take a while.

I stopped at the door to where Kayson was digging through various pieces of wardrobe.

"Uh, problem," I said.

"What's up?" he asked, not bothering to turn back.

"If I go around killing people while in this body won't it become pretty apparent that Evelyn Grayson is the one to hunt?"

"In that outfit, yeah," he replied.

"I mean, she's..." I paused and took a breath. "*I'm* apparently into philanthropy and stuff. I don't know the details, but rumor has it that this face is pretty well-known."

"Yep."

Kayson didn't seem to care one way or the other. That probably had to do with the fact that he wasn't the one who was a minor celebrity.

"So?" I pressed.

He stopped and looked back at me.

"You're in Black Ops, babe," he answered. "When we go do our gig, you'll be slapping your tat and resuming *you*."

Resuming me? What the hell did that mean?

"What?"

His shoulders slumped a bit.

"Okay, come in here and shut the door," he said, waving me over. I stayed put. He laughed. "You're clever, but I'm not planning to ravage you...yet." He'd added a wink. "Seriously, come in and shut the door. I want to show you something."

Since there was no sound of a zipper lowering, and recognizing that I was more than capable of taking care of myself, I complied.

Once in the room, he held out his arm to show me a tattoo that was exactly like mine, except for a few extra circles near his elbow.

"The large diamond near your wrist has a specific purpose," he explained. "When you press and hold it for five seconds, it will change the ink color. As soon as it does, you'll press it again and then run three fingers down the length of the tat."

I committed that to memory, thinking that it sure would be nice to have a user's manual for this and the connector. Why they provided these tools without any idea of how to use them was a mystery to me. How could a person be expected to do a job if they had no idea how to utilize all the tools?

"Is there a manual for all this stuff?" I asked.

"Yep," he replied. "Now, if you'll just go ahead and do what I said, you'll see why you don't have to worry about being recognized in public."

I sighed while pressing my finger on the large diamond shape at the top of my tattoo.

At the five second mark, the ink glowed a dark blue. After pressing the diamond again, it changed to green. As I slid three fingers from the top to the bottom, it slowly changed over to red.

Then I felt a momentary sense of nausea and the intense desire to step forward.

I did.

"Nice," Kayson said with the smile of a guy who'd just seen his first set of breasts.

I looked down, finding myself naked.

"Son of a bitch," I grunted, not bothering to cover myself up.

I knew I looked good, but I also knew that I was looking at my own body. Turning around, I saw the frozen image of Evelyn Grayson. She appeared to be stuck in suspended animation. Well, her body did anyway.

"The back's even better than the front," Kayson mused. "Of course, I *am* a bit of an ass man."

"More like an asshole," I countered, but I couldn't help but feel a bit aroused at the circumstance. A hit of horniness *had* left me the moment I stepped out of Grayson's shell, though. I was still a little hornier than usual, but leaving her dropped that a couple of notches. "So how does this work exactly?"

"Well," he said, standing, "you've already done step one. Next, I take off my clothes and we—"

"I'm talking about the separation I've just completed," I interrupted, throwing a thumb in the direction of Grayson. I pulled up my left arm and then looked back at the shell of a body behind me. "I still have my tattoo, but she does too."

"Nifty, eh?" he said, and then held up a hand at me. "Before you ask, I have no clue how that works."

"What about the connector?"

"*Should still work fine,*" he replied directly into my head. "*Again, no idea why.*"

The only thing I could think of was that the process of

possession wasn't simply a soul taking over a body. That's what most people thought, but it wasn't the case. It was more of a situation where a hellion or a demon merged with a body, almost like a dimensional shift that allowed us to blend. Once inside, we were the stronger of the two personalities, and could therefore take control. Sometimes, the merging was so deep that the possessor couldn't get out. If the host was killed, the underlying being would emerge.

Assuming that was the case, it meant that I'd really had two sets of tats and connectors when I was merged with Grayson.

I wanted to ask more questions of Kayson regarding the specifics of how the nanite technology managed this process, but the look on his face made it clear that he'd given me all he knew about that particular aspect of the process.

"Does she stay like that indefinitely or what?" I ventured.

"Three days," he answered. "After that, she fades away and that's that."

Three days was plenty of time to do most any job.

I nodded. "Does the transformation have to be done in this room?"

"Nope."

"Then why did you have me..." I paused and gave him a look. "You knew I was going to be naked."

"Duh," he laughed.

"Kiss my ass, Kayson."

"I'll RSVP to that invitation straightaway."

I put a hand on my hip, but instantly recognized that

my power move was doing nothing more than making his interest grow.

"I think I can take it from here," I stated.

"I don't think I can give it from here," he replied with a squint. "I mean, it's above-average and all, but I'd definitely need to be a little closer if I was…" He stopped, clearly catching the look on my face. "Oh, you meant finding something you want to wear, right?"

I pointed at the door. "Out."

"Right."

As soon as he exited the room, I began searching for an outfit. One of the things that Garrick had taught us during training was that green was a wise choice. Black was too obvious and blue was too flashy. Green, especially of the dark variety, went relatively unnoticed.

"Green it is," I said as I dug through the various outfits.

Once I'd picked everything out and put it on, I stepped in front of the mirror that stood next to the frozen body of Evelyn Grayson.

I looked good.

I'm not sure I'd call it something an assassin would wear, but that made it all the better since that was kind of the point.

A dark green shirt, dark jeans, a silver-buckled belt, and a long sleeve, green bolo jacket made up the breadth of the outfit.

It was nice to see my *actual* face, which was slightly more youthful than Grayson's, or maybe it just looked that way because of my olive skin. I also much preferred my purplish hair to her blond, and there was no topping the glowing blue eyes of a hellion when she was ready for battle, and I *was* ready for battle.

With a hint of menace, I summoned my dual blades.

Then, just to get the full effect, I raised my hands to the side and allowed a couple of energy orbs to form.

Okay, *now* I looked like an assassin.

CHAPTER 22

J walked out with a bit of a swagger, knowing that I looked good.

"Hubba hubba," Kayson said with fluttering eyelids. "You look seriously boneworthy."

"Well, aren't you the charmer?"

He scanned me thoroughly. "I daresay I prefer this look over the Grayson chick, but I wouldn't mind playing with both bodies."

With a smirk, I motioned back toward the dressing room. "Go ahead, I'm sure she won't mind."

"Sweet," he replied, taking a step toward the room.

I caught him by the jacket.

"You can't be seriously thinking about that," I laughed. "She's frozen in time and soulless, remember?"

"I've boned a number of soulless chicks," he replied.

"No, I mean she's *literally* soulless."

"Oh, right." He rubbed his chin. "Okay, fair enough. It's probably a bit too much, even for me."

The look on his face almost betrayed him. Was he just

toying with me? Was all of his bravado nothing but a ruse? The smug look he wore made me think that this was nothing but a game to him. The glimmer in his eyes didn't exactly belie my supposition either.

"Something tells me you're not the player you claim to be," I said as I walked toward Q's desk. "I think you're more talk than walk."

"You'd be wrong," Q breathed as he continued typing away at his workstation. "He's ever on the prowl."

"Well," Kayson jumped in, "I *am* a dog, so…"

"Anyway," Q said, after smacking down the enter key on his keyboard, "I have a plan for getting to Willow." He looked up and blinked a couple of times. "Wow."

I furrowed my brow at him. "What?"

"You look…" He cleared his throat and then refocused on his screen. "You look nice."

"Thank you," I replied, allowing myself a small grin.

It wasn't often that a vampire told you that you looked nice, unless you were another vampire, of course…or a fae, but that was expected. Not that I'd run into a lot of vampires in the Badlands. There were a few, sure, but they didn't much frequent the hellion areas.

"Hey," Kayson said, giving me a look, "I told you that you were boneworthy and you didn't thank me."

"Gee," mumbled Q, "I wonder why?"

"See?" Kayson said, pointing at Q. "Even he doesn't get why you didn't thank me."

Okay, so chivalry was not one of Kayson's better traits, but that honestly didn't bother me much. I liked his type. It fit the Guard more than Q. Garrick wasn't like him, no…at least not as far as sexuality was concerned. To be fair, it wasn't as if I'd ever seen Garrick in a situation like that, but my gut said that he hadn't been a womanizer. However, just like Kayson, Garrick had been rough, tough, and had a way of not mincing words. The rest of the Guard, men *and* women, were ever on the prowl for rut-partners, though...me included. So, while I appreciated the gentlemanly nature of Q, as it related to how I looked in my new outfit, my libido was more driven to find Kayson as the better suitor. It wasn't like I could really start a meaningful relationship topside anyway, so getting laid was probably my only physical outlet, aside from fighting, of course.

On top of that, it didn't seem like Evelyn Grayson had much in the way of permanent relationships. She had a fuckbuddy, but he'd died in the limo crash along with her. According to Cruze, she *did* have other friends with benefits. Maybe some of them would work out? That caused my mind to drift back to the naughty room at Grayson's place. I *could* use a whip, but I'd rather just get animalistic about things.

Another glance at Kayson told me that he would prove useful for animalism.

And, no, I don't mean that in the sense of him being a hellwolf.

Ew.

I mean it as him being a rogue.

He was my type. Tough, rugged, and irreverent. He didn't take shit from anyone, he said what was on his mind, he was rebellious, and I had the feeling that he would be one hell of a challenge in the sack.

Okay, I was *definitely* feeling more horny than normal here.

"Listen," I said, taking a step away so that I was able to face both my new partners, "does something happen that causes you to be a little more amorous when you transfer up here?"

"Topside?" asked Kayson.

"Yeah."

"I don't think so."

"It's the tattoo," interrupted Q, though he had returned to scanning his computer screen. "For every capability you have, the tattoo increases your libido some."

I scrunched my face and shook my head.

"That makes zero sense."

"Agreed," Q replied with a nod. "It's ridiculous and frustrating."

"Doesn't bother me at all," Kayson chimed in. "I kind of like it."

"You would," stated Q. He then glanced up at me. "It has something to do with how the tattoo interfaces with your physiology, the main system, and your connector. I don't know all the specifics, but everything pulses through your brain and nervous system. It all gets intensified because of this."

"Strange," I said as I studied my tattoo again. "It *did* seem to diminish when I exited Grayson."

"That's because you effectively have two complete PPD integrations running when you're inhabiting her body," Q explained. "One of them is yours directly, and the other belongs to Miss Grayson. When you are interconnected, it causes a doubling effect."

I nodded at him. "Plus, when I'm possessing her, everything else about us merges. She was pretty horny already, according to my cat, so mix that with my own hellion nature, add in a couple of PPD tattoos, and whammo."

"Your cat?" asked Kayson.

"Grayson's cat," I clarified.

"Ah." Kayson then jolted. "Grayson has a talking cat?"

Damn.

"Long story," I said, hoping that they didn't know much about hellions. "Let's just say that hellions are able to communicate with some animals."

It was a complete fabrication, and the questioning glance that Q gave me made it clear that he knew better. Kayson, though, either didn't know or didn't care. He just shrugged. My guess was that Q held back from challenging me on the point because he recognized that the less he knew, the less trouble he could get in if anything untoward unraveled due to the cat.

"Look, Eve," Kayson said gently as he walked over and put his hand on my shoulder, "I can only imagine that all of this is difficult on you. Being super horny all the time, I mean." His look of concern was oddly genuine. "Just know that I'm here for you, if you ever need anything."

I rolled my eyes and snorted. Then, I looked over at Q. "Does he ever give up?"

Q shook his head and pointed at his screen. "As I said before, I've gotten things worked out. Willow is in the northern point of the Crest. We should be able to transport close to where she is so we can avoid unnecessary confrontations."

"The Crest?" I asked.

"Underground area," Kayson answered as he dropped his hand from my shoulder. We both moved to look at Q's screen. So, he *could* be serious. "It's where supers hang out."

"Only if they're criminals," Q added with a healthy heaping of derision.

"You're a criminal, Q," Kayson countered. "Remember?"

To his credit, Q didn't retaliate. I could see that he desperately wanted to, but there was something about his demeanor that shifted a moment before he opened his mouth. Control? Had to be. Again, I wasn't super knowledgeable about vampires, but everyone knew how prim and proper they were capable of being... stereotypically speaking, anyway.

"If we transport here," he said, pointing to a cross section of the map, "we'll only need to navigate through one building, get to the basement, and climb down into the underground." He slid his finger to an empty area. "According to the data sheet that came in regarding the mission details, Willow and her guards will be here."

"But that's blank," I noted.

"Yes," agreed Q. "Any questions before we get started?"

I sighed. Clearly my point about it being blank wasn't going to be addressed.

Kayson and I moved back as Q got to his feet. He turned to give me another once-over and then frowned.

"Did you have her speak with Peggy?" he asked Kayson. "I don't see any—"

Kayson snapped his fingers and pointed at Q. "Forgot about that."

I glanced back and forth between my partners. "Peggy?"

"Our tech chick," Kayson replied, grabbing my wrist and dragging me behind him. He was a lot stronger than I would have guessed. "You'll like her."

"I'll wrap everything up here," Q called out after us. "We should be prepared to go in twenty minutes."

CHAPTER 23

You heard that you can trust no one, but to live like that is to live a life not worth living. Live with trust in your hearts. Just don't be foolish about it.

— GARRICK - HOUSE OF SINISTER

Since escaping topside, I'd experienced a number of new things. The smell, for one, but also possessing a normal's body for the first time, talking to a cat, getting a tattoo that embedded a connector in my brain, meeting a hellwolf, and being inducted into the Paranormal Police Department...though that seemed pretty loose, by my way of thinking.

So I shouldn't have been *too* shocked at meeting Peggy.

But I was.

Very, very shocked.

That had to do with the fact that Peggy belonged to a race that was equally as scarce as the hellwolf.

She was an orc. Tusks and all.

Not very many things intimidated me, but staring up at a seven foot block of muscle sent a shiver down my spine. She was a brownish green color with black eyes and ivory tusks that stuck up from the bottom of her mouth. Her arms were the size of Kayson's thighs. But there were a few things about her that confused me. First, she was wearing blue eye shadow, rouge, and bright red lipstick; second, she had on a pink outfit that hugged her every muscle; and third, she was wearing high-heeled shoes that had to have been constructed from titanium.

In a nutshell, she looked like a massive dude in drag.

"What's up, K?" she said in a surprisingly feminine voice.

"Hey, Pegs," Kayson replied as he leaned on the counter that separated us from what appeared to be a workshop. "Got a new recruit here."

"So I see," Peggy replied, clomping over and looking down at me. She sniffed the air. "Hellion. Interesting."

For some reason, that snapped me out of my sense of awe.

"The name is Evangeline," I stated somewhat defiantly.

"Peggy," she replied, sticking out her meaty hand. "You can call me Pegs, though. Everyone does."

That made me feel a bit snotty about how I had replied to her.

"Eve," I said more courteously while shaking her hand, which felt like it was easily three times the size of my own. "Sorry, I'm just a bit out of my element right now."

Peggy nodded at me. "It's not a problem. We've all been there, sweetie, haven't we, K?"

"Yep." Kayson turned toward me. "If it hadn't been for

Pegs, I would have died on my first mission. She hooked me up with a couple new enhancements that gave me additional speed and strength."

"Plus some healing," added Peggy. "It's all part of the gig. K was a little tougher than most of the supers who have passed through my doors, though. He was my first hellwolf. Not exactly a common breed topside."

"I could say the same about orcs," I stated, but then felt suddenly ashamed of myself. "Sorry, I didn't mean—"

She smiled. "No, you're right. Most of my kind are gone." She then glanced away for a second. "Hell, for all I know, they're extinct. I haven't been to the Badlands in forever."

Many people believed orcs to be extinct, but now and then one would show up in Infernal City. It was kind of like how people topside felt about Bigfoot. If you saw one, you *knew* they existed; if you hadn't seen one, you *knew* those claiming to have seen one were a bit nutty. Rumor had it that there were small bands of them living in the Dragon's Teeth mountains on the outskirts, hidden away so as not to draw attention to themselves. Orcs weren't exactly loved. I'd seen a band of them in person when I was younger, and even came face to face with one, but that was a long time ago and it clearly hadn't desensitized my nervous system at all. There was just something about standing in front of a creature that could crush you without even breaking a sweat that was innately terrifying.

Still, I couldn't help but feel bad for her. Even if she wasn't the only one left of her kind, she was most certainly the only one topside. Plus, based on the fact that she was stationed inside of a secret area in a movie theater, I couldn't help but imagine she felt isolated and alone.

"Are you ever allowed out of here?" I ventured.

"No," she replied, looking downcast. Then, she smiled, revealing some surprisingly nice teeth. "Fortunately, K takes me to the movies once a week, wining and dining me on hot dogs, nachos, and sodas."

I gave Kayson an impressed glance.

"What can I say," he said, "I've got a soft spot for muscular chicks."

"And a hard spot, too," giggled Peggy.

Ew.

My 'ew' quickly changed to one of disbelief. If I was hearing Peggy correctly—and I seriously had hoped that I wasn't—she'd just implied that she and Kayson had spent a little time in the sack. Now, I don't know a lot about orc physiology, but the sheer size of Peggy made me wonder about the 'size' of Kayson.

As if I wasn't horny enough already.

"Right," I said, and then cleared my throat. "Anyway, it's very nice to meet you, Peggy…erm, Pegs."

"And you as well, Eve."

Peggy then did something I really wasn't expecting. She reached over the counter with both arms, gripped me by my shoulders, and lifted me straight up, setting me on the counter as if I were a toddler.

"All right," she said, studying me from head to toe, "let's see what we have here."

I wasn't used to being scrutinized in such a way, but it

didn't feel threatening. If anything, I'd say that I felt like a vehicle that a seasoned mechanic was evaluating for parts.

"I'm assuming you have some form of magical weaponry at your disposal?" she asked. She must have noticed my shocked look, because she grinned and added, "We were made to watch documentaries about hellions when I was young, in case we ever had to go to battle with your kind."

"No shit?" I laughed. "We had to do the same for orcs."

Peggy nodded. "Makes sense. So much war and violence in the Badlands. I much prefer it up here, even if I am somewhat caged in this place."

Again, that seemed unfair. Necessary? Probably, but it still sucked.

"So," she asked again, "weapons?"

"Oh, yes," I answered as I summoned my blades.

"Ah," she said, impressed, "a dual-wielder. Yours was the kind most feared by my people. We have a tendency of using direct-attacks, which work better against single blades."

That was true with most foes. A dual-wielder who didn't have the proper skills was often weaker than someone who only drew a single blade, but in the right hands, such as mine, two swords were quite a challenge to defend.

"Were you helped to develop the dual summoning or were you born with it?" she asked, seeming sincerely interested.

"I was born with dual summoning," I answered Peggy, finally. I purposefully left out the part regarding the magic. Orcs were notoriously afraid of that. "I was one of the fortunate few."

"Lucky you," she said, almost sensing that there was more to my story than pure luck. "Well, the one thing we can do to improve your already fortunate skill is to give you enhanced speed and accuracy."

I tilted my head at her. "How?"

She smiled and clomped back toward her workstation, opening and closing drawer after drawer until she found what she was looking for.

"Here we go," she announced, walking back with a set of greenish-black armbands in her hands. "When you wear these, you'll not only find that your hands are more steady when using your blades, you'll also suffer less fatigue."

"Seriously?" I said as she affixed the first one. I felt an instant change in wrist strength. "Whoa."

"Even better," she added with a wink, "your magic ability just shot up about tenfold."

My jaw hung open. "You're kidding."

"Nope," she laughed, "but be careful. You're not a natural magic user, so you may need a little time to acclimate."

I nodded as I looked over the supple bracers.

"Nice."

"All right," Kayson said, "we should get going. Q's going to start bitching if we're not ready to walk out the door when he is."

"Tell him I said 'toodles,' will ya?" Peggy asked with a meaningful sigh.

I gave Kayson a questioning glance.

He shrugged in response.

"Will do, Pegs."

"Nice to have met you, Eve," she said, patting my hand before lifting me up and setting me back on the other side of the counter. "If you have any problems with those bracers, let me know."

"Thanks, Pegs," I said, feeling like I'd just met the first person in this entire mess that I could comfortably hang out with. Garrick's words regarding trust came back to me again. Yes, Peggy was an orc, but so what? Kayson was a hellwolf and Q was a vampire, and I trusted them, right? Okay, not really, but so far they hadn't done anything to warrant my blade, so that was trust enough. "And, listen Pegs," I added, "if you want to catch a movie together… you know, just us girls…let me know."

"That would be great," she said with a look of surprise. "K doesn't appreciate chick flicks."

Neither did I, but I also didn't have the heart to tell her that.

CHAPTER 24

*W*e stood around Quinton's desk, looking over his plan. There were drawings and timetables and even a tab labeled "contingencies."

"What the fuck is this?" Kayson asked between slurps of his mostly-empty soda.

Q looked up and frowned. "This contains the necessary details to ensure we have a successful mission. We go through this every time, as you may recall?"

Kayson grimaced. "We do?"

"Yes, we do," Q sighed. "You patently ignore it every time, of course."

"Ah, right! That's the part I remember." He expertly launched what remained of his drink into a trashcan across the room. "How about we just skip to that and go kill stuff?"

Q shut his eyes for a moment, looking as though he was doing his best to contain his angst.

I was kind of on the fence here. While planning was definitely something Garrick had drilled into the Guard during years of training, he was also a huge supporter of improvisation. There was only so much you could plan for, and usually those were only useful for larger attacks. Assassinations, or whatever it was we were supposed to be doing here, consisted of an individual or small teams. That meant over-planning was just going to tie our hands when reality hit. Hell, even large plans often consisted of breaking teams into manageable pieces that moved on a board in a macro capacity. It was up to the individual commanders to handle the tactical.

Still, having a general idea of what we were doing was smart.

"You may have noticed that we have a new person with us, Kayson?" Q chastised the hellwolf while motioning toward me. "Don't you think it would do her well to know the entirety of a plan so that she doesn't get herself, or either of us, killed?"

"I don't care if she gets *you* killed, Q," Kayson replied, "but I suppose I'd like to hang around a bit."

"Charming."

"I'd like to hear the details," I stated.

It wasn't an attempt to get on Q's good side or to get on Kayson's bad side. I just wanted to know what I was getting into here.

The fact of the matter was that I was new topside. I didn't know how things worked. And it didn't matter if topside *was* based on the Netherworld, things change over time. The majority of elements up here were designed on Netherworld Proper anyway, not the Badlands...except for the Strip in Las Vegas. Everyone knew that. But what was Los Angeles formatted after? Doubtful it was anywhere in the Badlands.

"You really want to know about this crap?" Kayson asked, looking both confused and disappointed.

"Yeah, you really do?" agreed Q.

I frowned at them both. "How long have you two been topside?"

"I dunno," Kayson answered. "Mmm...couple years, I guess."

"Thirteen years, seven months, and—"

"Right, right," I interrupted, waving at him, "I get it. The point is that you two know your way around here. I don't. Sure, I could just follow you two and kill stuff, but I'd rather have my wits about me when I'm here."

"Why?" asked Kayson.

"Because if you two get killed, where will that leave me?"

"Dead, too, probably."

"Agreed," Q affirmed, pointing at Kayson.

I hadn't known them very long, but it was pretty clear that they didn't agree on much. That added credence to them agreeing on the fact that if they died, I'd probably have perished alongside of them.

"Still," I pushed forward, "I'm of the mind that knowing something is better than knowing nothing. That said," I added while pointing at his documents, "you have clearly put far too much work into this, Q. We're just assassinating someone, right?"

He shook his head. "We are *not* assassinating someone, no. We are getting to Willow so that we may extract information from her. That is all."

Kayson and I shared glances. He looked downright pitiful, which I assumed had to do with the prospect that we weren't going to be killing our target.

"We're not killing anyone?" Kayson ventured, sounding almost pleading. "I sharpened my wrist blades and everything."

I gave him a look. "Wrist blades?"

"Yeah," he replied, brightening considerably. "Check it out."

Kayson pulled up the sleeves on his jacket, revealing a couple of metallic bracelets. They covered the top of his arm up to his elbow, but were mostly opened on the bottom. That worked out perfectly because he clearly needed access to his tattoo in order to move around properly and such.

With a smirk, he made two fists and then clanked the bracers together. A couple of blades shot out of the sides about four inches each, as another, wider blade shot straight forward, extending out over his hand. That one stuck out a solid inch beyond the extension of his fingers.

"Nice," I said with genuine admiration. "Has a bit of a Wolverine vibe to it."

"Love that guy," Kayson agreed with a nod. "These would be cooler if they were more like his, but they're still pretty sweet. You just gotta remember to put them away before taking a leak." His face paled instantly. "That is *not* fun."

I fought to keep from squinting at him.

"Right," I said. "Okay. Anyway, while I'm definitely not a fan of over-planning…"

"Thank the Vortex," Kayson mumbled.

"...I do think it's smart to have a solid *idea* of what we're getting ourselves into before diving in, so just share the highlights."

Q's face fell slightly, but he slowly pushed the contingencies document out of the way.

In some respects, I felt for the guy. He clearly enjoyed building grandiose plans. I assumed that came from his anal retentiveness. To not be able to enact those plans likely sucked, or at least to be able to share what he most assuredly considered "genius" with someone of like mind had to have made for a lonely time.

But I wasn't interested in the depths of strategy, and it was clear that Kayson wasn't either.

Plus, Q's attitude had been a bit abrasive since I'd met him. In other words, taking a few minutes to pretend to give a shit wasn't going to happen. He'd have to prove himself worthy of my sympathy before I gave it to him.

A vision of Garrick shaking his head at me came to mind. "Always use every advantage," he would have said, "even if it means doing something uncomfortable."

I'd lived those words enough during my time as a Guard to know that they made perfect sense. I just didn't like doing many of those things that were definitely uncomfortable.

"Listen," I said with some effort, "I'd be happy to dig into some detail with you, if you *seriously* think it will make our job go smoothly." I leaned in and looked him straight in the eye. "Can you honestly say that us planning every nuance is going to allow for fluidity if the shit hits the fan?"

"Well..." he started, but then let out a slow breath. "I can't say that for certain, no."

"I see," I said, pushing back away from the desk. Time to use some of Garrick's teachings. "But I'm guessing you *can* say that *some* of your plan will give us a better chance at success if we actually follow it, right?"

Q looked up, surprised. "Yes. I mean...absolutely."

"Then share those things with us," I said with as much enthusiasm as I could manage.

"Aw, fuck," Kayson groaned.

"*Only* those things," I added to Q. "That way we get to the job as smoothly as possible, get it done, and get back."

"Yes, yes," Q replied, his face almost shining as he pulled the papers apart and began to reorganize them. "I'll just need a moment to get everything situated."

With a sigh, I glanced over at Kayson.

He gave me a dark look and then shook his head. It was obvious that he was *not* a fan of my tactics, but I had the feeling that Kayson was the kind who flew by the seat of his pants a little too much. He was reckless. So was I, to a degree, but my gut said that Kayson took recklessness to a new level.

That sat me between the two of them.

"I'm going to get some fucking popcorn," Kayson grumbled as he stalked off.

"Hurry back," Q called after him. "I'll be done soon."

"Fuck off, Q."

That's when it hit me.

They'd both not only listened to my words, but they'd obeyed them. Q was paring down his plans so that we could have something more useful to work with, and

Kayson was putting aside his desire to just play everything off the cuff and instead take a little direction.

I'd just taken over as the leader of this little group. If Garrick had been there, he'd have been proud.

As for me, I wasn't exactly thrilled with the prospect.

CHAPTER 25

The walkway to the place Q had called the Crest was underground. We'd arrived via the portal, off in a side room that was full of boxes and junk. It looked like it hadn't been cleaned in years. That was probably a good thing, considering it best that nobody knew where your portal platform was. Not that it really mattered. The portal was at the back of the room behind a hidden zone that was further protected by a null zone and many wards. Anyone stupid enough to go this far back, without proper authorization, would get the hell shocked out of them.

Fortunately, my new tattoo gave me the authorization.

There were shops running the length of the corridor we were walking down. Everything from clothing to kitchenware was covered here. It reminded me of the shopping centers in the Badlands, though maybe cleaner.

Voices reverberated, bouncing off the high walls and polished floors.

The flow of shoppers was greater than I'd expected in

the supernatural community. I knew that there were a number of supers living topside, and many of them were clustered in the major cities around the world, but I hadn't expected there to be this many.

While I generally kept my magic low, I couldn't resist reaching out a little to see what types of people were actually up here.

The predominate race was vampire. That wasn't surprising, really. They were known to be somewhat prolific in all things business. The werewolf population wasn't too far behind, at least as far as the sample size of the mall was considered. The fact that they were living next to the vampires was interesting. Either the stories we'd been fed all our lives were wrong about their mutual hate, or they'd just learned to get along because they were afraid to lose their places topside.

Everyone knew the general rules regarding living up here. You played it smart, didn't make trouble, and returned for your reintegration cycles on time. If you didn't, the PPD would send a Retriever team after you. Retriever teams were notorious for shooting first and asking questions later. Assuming you were lucky enough to actually get retrieved, instead of killed, you'd end up undergoing a *full* reintegration, which I was told was the equivalent to being mentally dipped in acid, shaved with a rusty blade that would most assuredly nick your flesh from head to toe, and then dipped back in acid again. I'd never gone through even a basic integration cycle, seeing that hellions were not generally allowed topside, but the stories were enough to make me understand why people up here kept themselves in line.

But I hadn't really considered Retrievers as a point of concern...until now.

"Quick question," I asked as we continued our stroll toward the far end of the mall, "are we in any danger of Retrievers coming after us?"

Kayson grinned. "Scared?"

"More like worried," I answered. "There's already a line of hellions seeking to take me down. I could do without having Retrievers on my ass, too."

"You're fine," Q said before Kayson could continue his teasing. He pointed at my arm. "Our tattoos hide us from the main systems. Nobody knows you're here." He shot me a quick look. "Except for your hellion friends, of course."

That was a relief.

Hellions, I could deal with...mostly. Having to watch my back for a bunch of others coming after me, though? It was just too much. I was already struggling to come to terms with everything that had happened, and being topside was something I'd never even considered as a possibility. To say my plate was full was an understatement.

"*Okay,*" Q said through the connector as we closed in on the back wall, "*we'll be turning left up here. Act natural. No being mesmerized or anything like that, understand?*"

"*Got it,*" I replied.

"*Fuck you,*" affirmed Kayson.

We turned the corner and it took everything I had to maintain my cool.

There were armed soldiers lining the walls. All male. All shirtless. All incredibly gorgeous. I'm talking long hair, rippling muscles, tight pants that hid nothing.

"*Um...drool,*" I cooed.

"*Keep it in your pants, sister,*" Kayson laughed. "*They're all chained.*"

"*Chained?*"

"*Yeah,*" he replied. "*They've been connected to their mistress. She's the only one they'll bone. You wouldn't even be able to give them a halfy. Q might, though, just from suction alone.*"

"*What are you talking about?*" Q shot back. "*I have no interest in men.*"

"*So you're no longer going to GH Station to make a few dollars on the weekends?*"

"*No! ... I mean, I've never done that.*"

Kayson was all smiles.

"*GH Station?*" I ventured.

"*Glory Hole,*" Kayson replied. "*It's down on the other side of the mall.*"

"*Go there yourself a lot, K?*" Q quipped.

"*Pretty much every weekend, yeah,*" he answered like it wasn't a big deal. "*No dudes, though. I'm not like you, Q.*"

Q went to retaliate, but he just rolled his eyes instead.

"*Anyway,*" Kayson continued, "*these guys are balls deep in Willow, physically and mentally. It wouldn't matter if you were the hottest chick on the planet, they only have eyes for her.*"

He turned and studied my face for a few seconds and nodded.

I frowned. "*What?*"

"*Nothing,*" he said with a shrug.

"*What?*" I pressed.

"Just thinking that you've got a nice canvas," he replied, shrugging again.

"Canvas?"

"Face," he explained with a sigh.

"Okay...thanks?"

"No problem. If you're ever in the mood, let me know. I'd love to paint it."

"Gross," Q snapped.

I, on the other hand, nearly snorted out a laugh. Kayson was disturbing, bold, and more than a bit uncouth, but he was my kind of person. I much preferred people who were direct over those who were manipulative.

"I'll keep that in mind," I replied. *"I wouldn't mind painting your face either."*

Q audibly gagged at that, which only solidified the smile that Kayson and I were sharing.

Past the line of delectable males was the nightclub where Willow was purported to be hanging out in.

It was dark with flashes of light that matched the rhythm of the music. There were tables to the right and left, surrounding a dance floor in the shape of a horseshoe. Directly ahead, through the mass of dancing patrons, was a large bar. The bass was pumping so hard that it felt like it was pounding through my chest.

"Can we please focus back on what we're supposed to do here?" Q pleaded. *"I'd rather not throw up in the middle of a mission."*

He was right. As Garrick had always said, "Play was play, but work was work, and work always came before play."

I shook my head to put myself back into work mode as we reached the bar and leaned against it.

"*Sorry,*" I said. "*According to your plan, this Willow person is up those stairs and around the back of the bar.*"

"*She should be, yes.*"

"*Okay. Kayson's going to the left, I'm going to the right, and you're staying put down here.*"

"*Chicken,*" Kayson snarked.

"*I'll be keeping an eye on everything and letting you know if the guards start moving in,*" Q replied, clearly ignoring Kayson's teasing.

"*How will you let us know, exactly?*" asked Kayson. "*By running away at full-speed, I'm guessing?*"

"*It's not like he could really help us,*" I interjected before Q could respond, trying to regain some of the trust that Kayson had given me before I insisted we study Q's plans. "*I guess he could bring us water bottles or something...*"

Kayson was all smiles at that statement.

Q was not.

Keeping the balance between these two was going to be trying, but necessary.

"*Anyway,*" I continued, "*let's get this over with. I haven't killed anyone in a while and my swords are starving.*"

"*Wait!*" Q barked. "*We're not killing anyone.*"

"*Well,* you're *not killing anyone,*" Kayson argued. "*You've not got it in you...and this time I'm not referring to the GH Station.*"

"*I'm talking about us as a team, Kayson,*" growled Q.

"*You want to go to GH Station as a team?*" Kayson asked, looking confused. "*It's a little weird, and I'm damn sure not going to be on the opposite side of the wall from you, Q.*" He snuck me a glance. "*Her? Definitely. But not you.*"

I sniffed. "*The holes in the wall are big enough to put your face through, Kayson?*"

"*Well played,*" he answered with a satisfied smile. "*Well played, indeed.*"

"What can I get you?" asked a young bartender.

She was bubbly.

I don't like bubbly.

"Whiskey," I replied.

"*It's not like the whiskey you're used to drinking,*" Kayson warned. "*It's like water compared to the stuff in the Badlands.*"

"*I'll take my chances.*"

Kayson had grabbed a vodka and Q requested something called a Strawberry Daiquiri.

"*Dude,*" Kayson said with a groan, "*are you* sure *you don't spend time down at GH Station?*"

"*Anyway,*" Q snarled as the bartender set off making our drinks, "*we're not killing Willow. We merely want to get information out of her. That's our mission. Information gathering, only. No killing.*"

"*All right, all right,*" Kayson said. "*No need to get your panties in a bunch, dude.*"

Something told me that his plan wasn't going to work out so well. People didn't just generally spill their guts when you asked for secret information. They had a tendency of *not* speaking. How you got around that was to either take the time to befriend them, getting into their inner circle of friends, and then slowly bleed the intel you need, or you tortured the fuck out of them until they screamed out every last detail.

We clearly had no time for playing buddy-buddy with her, which left pointy objects and painful shocks.

That meant the guards—those mouth-watering, smoking hot guards—were bound to take notice.

"How do you expect us to get her to tell us what we want to know without using some kind of force?" I asked. *"Anything we do is going to cause those guards to flood back there."*

"Phrasing," noted Kayson as the bartender set our drinks down.

"That'll be thirty," she said, all smiles.

Kayson and I glanced over at Q.

He sighed and dug into his pocket to pay the woman, giving her thirty one.

"Wow," she said, her smile fading fast. "One whole dollar? I can retire in style now."

Q's face was wooden as Kayson and I giggled.

"Don't blame him too much, baby," Kayson said to her as he fished a twenty out of his pocket and set it in her hand. "He's got to save his money to buy a prime spot at the GH Station."

CHAPTER 26

Sometimes it's better to trust your eyes than to trust your gut.

— GARRICK - HOUSE OF SINISTER

I slipped up the stairs on the right side of the bar, feeling like I'd had nothing at all to drink.

Kayson was right about the whiskey. It wasn't very strong at all. I couldn't tell if they watered it down or what, but I'd need at least three times the amount I drank in the Badlands to catch a decent buzz off the stuff up here.

There were guards at the top of the steps, but they hadn't blocked my way. In fact, they barely even seemed to notice me at all. Whatever hold this Willow chick had on them was pretty heavy, because I looked pretty damn tight in my current outfit.

I glanced across to the other side and found that Kayson had gotten through without a fuss either.

If nothing else, Willow was clearly pretty lax on her own personal security. That could have been due to the fact that she was high up in whatever crime syndicate we were infiltrating. I was still a bit fuzzy on the details regarding all of it. Mostly because I honestly didn't give a shit. If I was getting poised to take over a kingpin or something, the story would have been different, but jumping out and taking care of business as a cop wasn't enough to make me push the envelope.

Cop.

It felt seriously odd to think of myself in that way. I was a Guard, not a cop. It was the same thing in many ways, but not all. Cops tended to protect the general public from the criminal element. A hellion Guard was there to protect their House from other Houses, or from traitors to the House. If an official from another House was getting her ass whipped in the middle of the street, I would feel zero obligation to intervene. I probably still *would*, depending on the circumstances, but it wasn't like it'd be my job to do so. As a cop, though, I'd have no choice.

But that's where this job was even stranger.

According to Q and Kayson, and based on the inferences made by the Directors, I wasn't just a standard cop. Undercover? Maybe. Honestly, though, it felt like the Directors needed a small group of people to handle their dirty work and the only way they could slide that past whatever committees voted on shit like that required that proper procedures got followed. So, based on what little information I was working with, I guessed that through some fucked-up loophole, the Directors came up with the idea to slap a badge on a few killers and call them cops.

"*Got a question,*" I said through the connector. "*Am I supposed to show this woman a badge and tell her I'm a cop? If so, I'm going to have to borrow one of your badges...or just let Kayson do it.*"

"*We're not really cops,*" Kayson replied. "*We're assassins who happen to work for the PPD.*"

"*That's not entirely accurate,*" Q countered. "*We are sanctioned by the Paranormal Police Department. Therefore, we are cops. We don't, however, carry badges, nor do we introduce ourselves as being police.*"

"*And why do you think that is, Q-hole?*"

Q didn't dignify Kayson's question with a response.

"*All right,*" I continued, "*so what do we say when we get to her?*"

"*Nothing,*" Kayson answered. "*We just kill her and get the fuck out.*"

"*No, you do not,*" Q growled. "*This is not an assassination mission, Kayson. I honestly don't know how many times I have to tell you that.*" Kayson was giving me the thumbs up, smiling from ear-to-ear as Q continued his tirade. Obviously, the hellwolf was just having fun winding up the vampire. "*Again, and I say this emphatically, we are not here to assassinate anyone. Please tell me you both understand that, entirely!*"

"*I got it,*" I said, feeling a little bad for the vampire. The guy had to have been developing an ulcer. At the same time, playing with Kayson was the most fun I'd had since being up here. "*We're not here to gather information. We're here to assassinate Willow.*"

"Right," Q rasped. Then, followed up with, *"What? No! We are* not *here—"*

"Q, Q, Q," I interrupted him with a laugh, *"we're just messing with you."*

"Yeah, man," Kayson chuckled. *"Lighten the fuck up already."*

The channel went silent as we closed in on a nice leather couch that housed who had to be Willow.

The instant I saw her, I realized why the shirtless guys had zero interest in me. She was drop-dead gorgeous. Sleek black hair hung down the sides of her perfect face. Her eyes shone like diamonds, literally. She either had magic flowing through her veins, or she was wearing some type of contact lens that gave the affect. Her lips were full, looking like a couple of pillows that I was sure Kayson would love to sleep on. I wouldn't have minded either, if I was being honest. Her outfit was pure white, and it fit just as tightly as the ones she'd made her manservants wear. She was filled out in all the right places and didn't seem to have an inch of fat anywhere else…except those lips.

I shook my head, finding myself captivated by her beauty. It was obviously going to take a lot of work to keep my enhanced libido under control, and at this point I wasn't even in Evelyn Grayson's body, where I was getting an even higher dose of horny.

"Damn," Kayson said as he stood in front of her, looking like he was near drooling. "Now *that's* a canvas I wouldn't mind painting."

"Excuse me?" Willow said in a smooth voice.

"Ignore him," I said, drawing her attention over to me. "He's a perv."

"I like pervs," she replied, raising an eyebrow in the process.

"Oh."

She studied us both for a moment as a little pixie flew over and settled on her shoulder. He stood about six inches tall, had tiny wings, and was wearing a stretchy outfit that was similar to Willow's. The nub of a tiny member was straining against the fabric like the tip of a pin. Not impressive from my vantage point, but I had the feeling that female pixies might have been rather impressed.

I'd never been a fan of pixies. They weren't trustworthy. They *were* hilarious at times, especially their use of colorful language. The way they called people names was a thing of art.

"Who are these pee hole pirates?" he asked.

"I haven't the foggiest," Willow replied, after taking a sip from a dark liquid she'd been holding. I was entranced at the sight of her lips on the rim of the glass. "Well?"

I blinked a few times.

Damn, this woman had some serious power.

"Uh…we're cops…I mean assassins…I mean cops who are assassins."

Kayson squinted over at me. *"Well-played, rookie. I'll take it from here."* He cleared his throat. "What my partner is trying to say, Willow, is that we're here to assassinate you. I mean, uh…to question you."

"Yeah, that was better," I chided him.

Willow set the glass down and leaned back in the chair as a smirk appeared on her face.

"So you're here to assassinate me?" she asked. "Have you seen the mass of men I have as protection?"

"You make them wear protection?" Kayson asked. Then, he looked up. "Oh, wait...*as* protection. Sorry. Just didn't seem to make any sense that—"

"Silence," commanded Willow.

"Yep," agreed Kayson, putting his hands respectfully behind his back.

I thought that strange until I noticed that my fingers were interlaced behind my back as well.

She was controlling us. I wasn't sure how, but I assumed it had something to do with magic. Too bad for her that I had a pretty decent ability to use the arts as well.

I cleared my head, remembering who I was... remembering the years I'd spent training, peeling back the layers of the onion that represented my life until I'd dealt with every issue that marked my youth. I'm not saying that my training represented a complete cure. Far from it. If anything, it had fucked me up even more. But what I *did* get out of it was the ability to see beyond the layers of fog that people put up as a front as they presented themselves to the world.

The woman in front of me was not just a woman, and she wasn't using 'magic' as her means of controlling everyone...technically. It wasn't the magic of a wizard or a mage or a witch, anyway.

We were being drawn in by a succubus. It explained all the men under her control. It explained how Kayson was drooling, though something told me that most any woman could have that affect on him. It also told me how she was gripping my sexuality in her snare.

It was simply in her nature.

Lucky bitch.

I broke the clasp of my fingers and moved them back around to the front.

Her eyes sparkled for a moment and she looked up at me with renewed interest.

"What are you?" she asked.

"Hellion," I replied before I could stop myself.

Apparently, knowing what she was didn't mean I'd be able to fully control my response to her.

"Interesting," Willow whispered, leaning forward with a devious grin. "Very interesting."

"Shit," I hissed, recognizing precisely what she meant by that. I summoned my swords and announced, *"Plan B, guys."*

"Plan B?" shrieked Q. *"There is no Plan B!"*

"There is now!"

CHAPTER 27

I'd battled against the best in my day, but this was the first time I was fighting someone who was seriously messing with my head.

My blades were out and I was poised to strike.

I just couldn't do it.

Her smile was something I wanted to just fall into, to touch…to serve.

The new bracers Peggy had made kept my arms so steady, they felt almost robotic. Under normal circumstances, I could have struck her down with a perfect arc, without even a millimeter of wavering.

But…I couldn't.

"What the fuck?" I bellowed, shaking my head fast as I grimaced.

Willow laughed and snapped her fingers, summoning a couple of her guards to come and destroy me and Kayson.

Three from each side moved from the walls, sliding their weapons out and gripping them firmly.

Yeah, I know…phrasing.

"Kayson," I barked, kicking him in the side just as one of the musclebound guys swiped straight down with his sword, missing the hellwolf by millimeters. "Get your head in the game, dipshit!"

I knew full well that was easier said than done, but as long as neither of us let our eyes sink into the depths of Willow, we'd have enough focus to kick some ass.

The problem was that I was far more interested in jumping in the sack with these guys than I was in killing them.

Until the first piece of steel slid across my bicep, that is.

There was something about getting cut by someone who was interested in killing you that provided a new perspective on things. This was especially true to a warrior who prided herself on not getting cut at all.

Translation: I got pissed.

"You fucker," I spat, dropping to one knee while sending my blade directly through his gorgeous chest.

I released that sword and spun, slicing the second one through the guard who was trying to sneak up on my right. It cut through his stomach, showing me parts of him that were far less than sexy.

The first guy I'd stabbed was falling backward, succumbing to the finality of the steel that had pierced his heart.

I grabbed the pommel of the blade and held it firm as gravity did the job of removing it fully from his corpse.

That brought me to the third guard.

One might assume that he would have seen how easily I'd dispatched his pals and gotten the hell out of there, but the look in his eyes told a different story.

Devotion.

Willow had this guy, and all of them, so wrapped around her finger that it was likely they'd walk right into a shredder if they believed it would please her.

To bad for him, I was that shredder.

With my three down, I turned to find that Kayson had already wasted the three who were after him, as well.

Willow had clearly not expected our level of capability, since she was still seated on the couch and her face was not holding that same confidence it'd held moments before.

The pixie had wisely left the scene.

"*What are you two doing back there?*" screamed Q through the connector. "*The guards are running back toward you!*"

"Shit," I grunted, glancing over at Kayson.

He sighed and reached out, sticking the point of his sword on Willow's neck. "Stop them or I'll kill you."

She regained some measure of control as she looked up into his eyes.

"You wouldn't actually hurt me," she cooed, "would you?"

Guards poured in from either side and they were charging directly at us.

"Kayson?" I said, my adrenaline starting to flow. "Kayson?"

Nothing.

We were seconds away from being sliced and diced.

"KAYSON!" I bellowed one last time as I grabbed his elbow and pushed it forward with all my might.

The sword pierced Willow's throat and pushed all the way through, sinking into the leather couch that she sat upon.

We fell forward on her as she gurgled her last and died.

I cringed, knowing full well that the battle wasn't over. Her glistening gladiators would likely be even more pissed now than they were before.

But the air had stilled and the sound had stopped.

I peeked back to find the men had all lowered their weapons. The looks on their faces weren't ones of anger or concern, they were of confusion. Kayson, too, looked baffled as he stared down at the body of Willow.

"What happened?" he asked.

"Yes," Q growled from in front of us, "what the hell happened?"

He had obviously come back to check on things firsthand, though I couldn't fathom why. He had to have known that there was a fight going on, and it wasn't like he could have done much to support us, except maybe act as a shield for a couple of seconds.

The sounds of clanging steel filled the room as the guards dropped their swords and began walking from the room.

That's when it hit me.

I looked back down at her, finding myself in awe of the power she'd had.

"She was a succubus," I explained to Q.

"So?"

"So that's why she was able to control everyone in here."

"Again," he reiterated, "so?"

I stood up and grabbed at the cut on my bicep. It stung.

"She was using the same power on me and Kayson," I stated. "It was twisting us and we were losing ourselves. When I went to break free of her grasp, she summoned the guards to kill us both."

"Again...so?"

I frowned at him. "You *are* a dick, aren't you?"

"Told ya," Kayson sighed as he pushed the hair out of Willow's eyes. "Such a shame." He then stood up and stuck his boot on her forehead and pulled his blade out of her throat. "She had such a perfect canvas."

I rolled my eyes at him and then looked down at Willow again.

She *did* have one hell of a canvas.

"So now what?" I asked, fighting to rip my head back to reality.

"Now we have to go back and tell the Directors that you two idiots failed," Q stated. "I'm sure they'll be incredibly happy to learn about that."

"Says the guy who sits comfortably at the bar drinking a Buttfairy Daiquiri."

"It's a Strawberry..." Q stopped and grunted. "Let's go."

That's when I noticed something fluttering near the back of the room.

"Wait a sec," I said, holding up my hand. "I believe we may be able to get that information yet."

I knew that pixies were fast, and I also knew that they could be pretty vicious. Seeing that this one was part of the crime syndicate that Willow was involved in, I imagined he could be quite a handful.

Magic was not something I enjoyed calling on, unless it was absolutely necessary, but seeing that we had taken down the woman we were supposed to have been questioning, I felt as though I had little choice.

Summoning energy, I flicked my wrist, sending a snare spell at the pixie with such speed that even he couldn't escape its grasp.

"What the shit?" he yelped as I reeled him in from across the room. "Let me go, you ball draining slut!"

Kayson smiled. "I like him."

"I bet you'd like my full eighth of an inch in your mouth, too, wouldn't you?" the pixie said.

"I like him, too," Q said, immediately after the insult.

The pixie spun around and looked at him. "You look like you'd prefer eight inches."

Q jolted, Kayson laughed, and I got down to business.

"Listen to me, you little shit," I said, staring darkly at the pixie, "you're going to give us the information that we want, or I'm going to send so much power through this connection I have with you that you'll cook from the inside out."

His eyes went huge. "Like the time those bastards down at The Eatery stuck me in the microwave? Barely made it out of that alive. Took two healers an hour to fix my insides, and that was only after being in the damn thing for five seconds!"

That sounds less than fun.

"Talk, little man," I said.

"About what, Queen of the Dipshits?" he shot back. "It's not like you've asked me anything specific!"

"Oh, right," I coughed. "Q?"

"Who is your boss?" Q asked, though he seemed like he would have rather gotten us in trouble with the Directors.

The pixie pointed at Willow.

Q took a deep breath. "Who was *her* boss?"

"Your mom?"

I sent a little shock through the connection.

"Ouch! Fucking titty twisters with jizz on top!" He glared at me. "Don't do that again!"

"Answer the questions and I won't," I replied, giving him a look that explained I was quite happy to send shock after shock until we got what we wanted. "Who was Willow's boss?"

Pixies rarely looked concerned, at least not the ones I'd seen over my years, and that included the documentaries we'd had to watch during training. They looked angry, jovial, and oddly menacing, but concern was not a common visage.

"If anyone finds out I told you that," he said, pulling at his collar, "they'll do stuff to me that will make your little shocks seem like loving caresses."

"And if you don't tell us, you'll die," I pointed out.

"I think I'd rather do that," he admitted. "Seriously, these guys are wicked as fuck." He pointed down at Willow. "She was a perv to the extreme, but she treated me decently. Except for that time she…"

"What?" asked Kayson.

"It only happened once, but…"

"What?" Kayson asked louder.

"She stopped because she finally believed that I couldn't make myself vibrate."

"Ew," the three of us said in unison.

"Anyway," he continued, "if I tell you three sponge mops who her boss is, and she finds out, I can't even imagine what they'll do to me." He took a deep breath and looked me square in the eye. "Go ahead and kill me. It'll be easier that way."

The little creep was either calling my bluff or he was serious. Based on what I knew about people in the higher levels of the hellion Houses, though, I had a feeling he was telling the truth. People that high up in power were often twisted. Not all of them, obviously, and many of them hadn't started out like that, but power has a way of bending the mind.

"What if we give you our word that you'll never be mentioned?" I asked.

"Yeah," Kayson agreed, slapping my arm. "It's not like we know your name or anything."

"Hal."

"Hmmm?"

"Hal," the pixie said again, looking at Kayson. "My name is Hal."

"Great," Kayson replied. "Now we know your name."

Hal facepalmed.

"Well, Hal," I stated again, "what if we promise not to say a word about who you are?"

He looked up at me. "You honestly expect me to trust you, lady?"

"Well, let's just say that I wouldn't go out of my way to see if you vibrated like some people in this room."

He cracked a smile at that. "Good to know."

"Also," I added, "you know something about me that I don't want revealed to anyone. I tell on you, you tell on me." I leaned in. "That goes both ways, too."

"Q does that," Kayson chimed. We looked over at him. "You know, goes both ways."

"I do *not*."

Hal giggled a bit at that. "Okay, I like you fuckers. Don't know why, but I do." He met my eyes again. "We've got a deal. I won't say anything about you if you don't say anything about what I'm going to tell you." He wagged a finger at me. "But if you're lying, just know that I'll scream your name as they're ripping my wings off and shoving the rest of me up their asses."

"Ew," said Kayson.

"I'm serious."

"About them shoving you up their asses?"

"No…" Hal paused. "Well, *yes*, actually…but I meant the bit about giving away her secret." He quickly motioned at everyone. "I'll make damn sure every one of you is fingered."

"That's a perk for Q."

"Will you *please* shut—"

"Guys," I interrupted, shooting them a look. "Hal is trying to tell us something here, remember?"

Q sneered at Kayson, who merely grinned in response. It was honestly like having a couple of kids in the backseat of a car who relentlessly teased each other. Actually, I suppose it was more like one kid who tortured the other.

Regardless, I was getting damn close to pulling the damn car over and tanning both their backsides.

"Sorry, Hal," I stated. "We agree to your terms. Now, who was Willow's boss?"

"Macy Bale," he whispered.

I released the containment field.

CHAPTER 28

*A*ndras sat at the desk in his chambers, waiting for good news.

He was the leader of the task force for House Varaz, which was the primary House responsible for the Rite of Decimation enacted against Sinister. It was he who had convinced the high elders to conspire with Houses Mathen and Tross. He was also the architect behind the convergent plan.

All had gone well, up until the point that one of the Guards from House Sinister had fled the scene. Not that Andras was really surprised by her cowardly act. She was not royalty, after all.

Still, in his estimation, a Guard of any worth would have stayed on to fight.

Andras had never been in the Guard, nor had he partaken in the killings. He'd been trained in battle just like everyone in Varaz, but he found the one-on-one act distasteful. His was a mind created to move pieces on a board. Setting him as one of the moving pieces made little sense. This became apparent when he was just a boy. His teachers would chastise him constantly about his poor technique with the blade, but they'd heap praise on his shoulders regarding his strategic maps. He had even received the highest honor in Varaz for developing an attack plan that rallied the Badlands during the Old War. Ultimately, that war had been lost, but only because the older generals hadn't listened to Andras. They were jealous old fools who were incapable of bowing to a superior planner simply because of his age.

But that was when Andras was just a boy. Those old generals had since died off, mostly from poisoned blades to the back, and Andras had taken the spot of primary architect. He'd since learned to watch his own back.

A knock came at the door.

"Yes?"

A young servant stepped partly into the room, having been trained to know better than to enter fully.

"Moloch has returned, my lord," the boy announced.

"Send him in," Andras replied, feeling somewhat worried.

The oracle had not updated the map to show that House Sinister had fallen to its last person. According to the readouts he was seeing on his globe, there was still one living member.

He ran his hand over his stubbled head and prepared himself for the worst of news.

Another knock came, followed by Moloch walking into the room and bowing.

"My lord."

"Moloch," Andras replied. He then motioned for the assassin to sit. "What is your status?"

"We lost her," Moloch answered, his voice laced with venom. "She slipped into hiding after dispatching three of my men. Well, one was killed by a flamebeast that was called upon by—"

"Trivialities," Andras stated, waving his hand. "Do you have a bead on her?"

"I left Craff topside to search around," Moloch answered, "but I could use more soldiers to make—"

"You'll have three in total," Andras interrupted, his voice calm. "Your current one from Varaz, one from Mathen, and one from Tross."

The look on Moloch's face was priceless. He had obviously despised the concept of sharing the glory of killing the final Sinister House member with soldiers not from his sect. Andras understood this on an intellectual level, but since he was not one who cared about the House itself, he couldn't fathom the blow to Moloch's patriotism.

Andras was more interested in winning, no matter the cost, and no matter who the pieces on the board represented.

Regardless, he was currently facing a wrinkle in his plan.

It wasn't as though he hadn't expected *some* people from Sinister to attempt to flee. Being hunted has a way of making a person seek escape. The issue was that he hadn't anticipated anyone heading topside. He'd placed soldiers along the wall to Netherworld Proper, had sentries seated on the Dragon's Teeth mountains, and even had multiple members of Infernal City's mafia on payroll in case anyone from Sinister happened to be spending time on the Strip.

Topside, though?

Unexpected.

The rarity of a hellion going topside was such that it shouldn't have even been a possibility, and if it hadn't been for the Forbidden Loch, it *couldn't* have been a possibility. Something scratched at the back of his head to inform him that such assumptions were for lesser strategists. He closed his eyes for a moment to acquiesce to his own logic. Of course there were other ways someone could travel topside, if they were clever enough.

Ego had always been an issue with Andras. He'd toiled away to correct that flaw since his youth, but it was ever the challenge, especially when faced with fools like Moloch.

"I assure you that we do *not* need the help of Mathen and Tross, my lord." Moloch had stated his point through clenched teeth. "We are quite capable on our own. If I could just have more assassins from our own House, I can—"

"You can what, exactly?" interrupted Andras with a raised eyebrow. "It seems to me that your proof of capability became questionable when you arrived at my door to inform me of your failure to catch and kill a mere peon."

Moloch twitched, but wisely held his anger.

"She may not be royalty, sir," he said coolly, "but she is clearly well-trained."

Andras sniffed at that statement, knowing fully that

Moloch had just moved the bishop to a place on the board where the king had become exposed.

"Better trained than you and your team, Moloch?" he asked, finally.

"Of course not, my lord," Moloch replied, as if slapped.

"You have just admitted to underestimating her ability, no?"

"I…well…"

Moloch trailed off.

"And you *did* come to request more troops, yes?"

"I did, my lord, but—"

"Which I find baffling, Moloch," Andras barked as he rose from his desk and pointed fiercely at the assassin. "If you and your goddamn crew are so much better trained than a pissant from the House of Sinister, why the fuck are you here asking for *more* soldiers?"

Moloch had leaned back, looking almost afraid at the outburst.

There was no possible way that Andras could best the man in even the lightest of physical battles, but Andras held rank and that was something respected in the Houses. Moloch wouldn't dare lay a finger on him, unless he was in the market for a year-long stint of horrific torture, followed by a certain trip to the Void. So he reacted precisely as a soldier should react when his leader screamed at him.

"You are out of your league in your attempt to combat wits with me, boy," Andras added as he returned to his seat. "You *will* take the people I assign from the Houses who share in the Rite of Decimation, and you will treat them with the respect and honor that they deserve. If I hear anything counter to that happening, your life and the lives of your entire line will be forfeit."

Moloch swallowed hard, but said nothing.

"Get out of my sight, Moloch," Andras commanded as he turned back to stare at his spherical map, "and don't return to me without completing your mission."

CHAPTER 29

*W*e'd gotten back to the theater and sat around waiting for the Directors to arrive. I kept the green outfit on, seeing no reason to change until jumping back into Grayson's body.

"Hey," said Kayson, leaning over from his chair, "thanks for shoving my sword into that chick's throat." He paused and grinned. "Heh…you know what I mean."

I smirked back. "Yeah, no problem."

"I don't mind a little role-playing," he continued, "but that succubus had some mean skills."

"You knew she was a succubus?"

"Duh," he replied, giving me a look. "Wait…you didn't?"

I shook my head. "Not at first, no. I'm not exactly what you would call a world traveler."

"Right on."

"You shouldn't have killed her," Q chimed in from his little desk. "We were specifically told to get information from her only."

Kayson and I shared an eye roll and a sigh.

We both knew that there was no point in arguing with our neighborhood vampire. He was by-the-book. If the Directors told him to drink one-eighth of a beer, he'd drink *exactly* one-eighth of a beer.

The boxes hummed a few seconds later, letting us know that the Directors had arrived. I couldn't help but wonder if they listened in prior to making themselves known. Not that it would have mattered to me, but some of the things Kayson and I said would definitely have ruffled Q's feathers if the Directors heard our words.

"What is your report?" asked Leighton.

I *did* appreciate the lack of pointless pleasantries...and the nice leather seats.

"We have the name of the boss Willow was working for, sir," Q answered, "but I would be derelict in my duties if I didn't mention that Kayson killed the woman."

"Dick," Kayson whispered.

"Unfortunate," Leighton said.

"And not prescribed by the mission details," grumbled Abner.

Kayson put up his hands, looking and sounding somewhat like Jeff "The Dude" Lebowski. "Yeah, well, shit happens, man."

"That will tack another few months to your sentence," Simone stated as a look of serene pleasure filled Q's face.

"Wait a sec, here," I piped up. "Kayson's blade went through her neck, but *I* was the one who shoved his arm. He couldn't do it because he was under the spell of a succubus."

Q's face fell slightly.

Good.

Dick.

"I'm not sure how things worked here before I arrived," I continued, "but if you're just taking the word of this asshole and not putting it into context of the reality of things…well, then you guys are fucked up."

"Pardon me?" Leighton's voice was dark.

While it probably wasn't the best move I'd ever made, I kept going. "I don't know what the hell you guys actually do for a living, but I spent years in the Guard. Plans change based on circumstance. You wanted us to get information. We did. Yeah, we weren't supposed to kill Willow, but that's where things went south. She was a succubus, and a damn powerful one." I paused to let that sink in for a second. "While Q sat comfortably away from the action, I was with Kayson facing down a real threat. If we hadn't fought back, you'd be staring at an impotent vampire who would be babbling about how your other two 'officers' were killed and there was no word on who Willow's boss actually was."

Q spun around at my comment about his being impotent. I hadn't meant it the way he likely thought I'd meant it, but then again…maybe. I'd tried to be cool with him, but I wasn't a huge fan of being thrown under a bus, especially after I'd tried to work with the guy.

"She speaks the truth," said Simone before anyone else could talk. "I knew Willow personally. She was quite formidable." There was a low, sad exhale. "She'll definitely be missed."

"No arguing that," I agreed. "It took everything I had not to fall completely under her spell."

Kayson was regarding me with a strange look, but he gave me a short nod.

"Fine," Leighton said. "We will accept that the mission parameters were unable to stay intact *this* time, but I do demand that everything is done to ensure that we keep things on track in the future."

"Agreed," said Abner. "We do not make rules simply because they're easy to make. Everything we do is carefully orchestrated to ensure the Black Ops version of the Paranormal Police Department remains well hidden."

"Just like the identity of its members," concluded Simone.

I got it.

If we kept stepping out and doing shit that was beyond the agenda, a light would shine on us. That, in turn, would out me to the Houses that were trying to finish the job against my House. In other words, keep my head down, keep my mouth shut, and do exactly the job I was told to do.

Too bad I wasn't someone who worked well like that.

Fortunately, it was only a year.

One year.

I just had to survive long enough to get back to the Badlands and take down the leaders of Houses that came after mine...the bastards who killed Garrick. When that day came, and I saw the blood spilling from those men and women, dealing with the shit I was faced with now would be completely worth it.

Besides, I had a pretty good gig here.

My initial expectancy was that I'd be living like a homeless person for the next year, roving all over the place while trying to avoid being killed by assassins. Instead, I was living the life of a wealthy playgirl, and playing the role in a secret organization in the PPD where I got to kill naughty pricks. All in all, I'd actually been dealt a decent hand...assuming you didn't consider the fact that my entire world had been ripped from me by Varaz, Mathen, and Tross.

So, yeah, I'd play the game as best I could.

But I wasn't stupid.

I wasn't going to just lay my life on the line to make sure that mission parameters weren't messed up, no matter what the Directors did. If they turned me in, I'd run. If they sent Q and Kayson after me, I'd kill them both in a heartbeat...especially Q.

My duty was to House Sinister first, not the Directors.

No, not even that was true.

My *first* duty was to the man who saved me from a shit life.

My first duty was to Garrick.

CHAPTER 30

Duty before drink. Duty before love. Duty before life. If duty does not call, however, then drink like your life depends on it and rut like it's your last day of breath.

— GARRICK - HOUSE OF SINISTER

*W*hen we walked out of the theater, I was fully on the side of telling Q to go fuck himself.

Kayson had warned me that the vampire would be in it for himself, which I supposed I should have guessed being that Q was a vampire! But I hadn't guessed it. To me, when you were on a team, whether by choice or not, you had each other's backs. That's how it worked. You didn't look for opportunities to screw your team members over. You didn't seek ways to better your position on the team by stepping on heads. And you sure as hell didn't throw a team member under the bus just to score points with the boss!

"I will be working to—"

"Fuck off, Q," I said, spinning on him. "You're a baby's dick. Plain and simple."

"Excuse me?" he replied, looking affronted.

I got nose to nose with him. "You're goddamn lucky I don't strap on a wooden dildo and chest fuck you right now."

To my surprise, Kayson pulled me back. He was laughing, but he was also physically insistent.

"Okay, okay," he chuckled. "Q definitely deserves an ass kicking...pretty much always, but how about you and me go grab a drink somewhere and leave him to all the paperwork that we don't want to deal with?"

Paperwork?

That was a term that was more terrifying than most.

It was a fitting punishment for us to leave Q to whatever paperwork was required in this job, too, but something told me that the vampire saw the concept differently. He was so anal retentive that he probably got aroused at the thought of paperwork.

"Fine," I replied, but shook Kayson away and stepped up to Q again. "One of these days we're going to be out in the field and you're going to be pinned down. When that day comes, I'll remember this day."

I gave him a shove and then turned to head back to Grayson's body.

Kayson was hot on my heels, giggling the entire time. Q wisely said nothing.

"Everything go okay?" asked Peggy, giving me a concerned look.

"It's just Q," Kayson replied, before I could get started.

"Ah, right," the orc nodded. "Say no more. He can be a bit of a pain sometimes. Nice enough guy, once you get to know him, but it's pretty clear that he'll do whatever it takes to get out of this outfit and back to his normal life."

"I'm not so sure he's going to live that long," I pointed out.

With that, I pushed into the changing room, after first holding up a hand in Kayson's face to let him know that he wouldn't be joining me this time.

Evelyn Grayson's body stood right where I left it...not that I'd expected it to move. I quickly disrobed, hanging up my new outfit before stepping over and merging back into Grayson.

The feeling was somewhat different than when I'd originally possessed her back at the limo. For one, this body was fully healed, except for the few scrapes and bruises I'd allowed so that those in the real world wouldn't get suspicious. More, though, was the sense of familiarity. I'd only been using the body for a couple of days, so I wasn't one hundred percent used to it just yet, but it was better. Still, it wasn't nearly as comfortable as my normal self. The one thing I could have done without, though, was the damn horniness that her genetic makeup added to my own horniness.

I knew that the PPD tattoo had made matters worse, though that still seemed really strange to me, but it was that damned succubus that had really turned my screws. Killing her was such a damn shame. Necessary, sure, but still sad. Interestingly, though, Grayson's demeanor, genetics, and the little sex room she had back at the house was enough to make me think she wasn't far from Willow.

But there was one more thing that pushed my arousal even further...fighting.

Maybe that's odd or maybe it's just the animalistic response to being near death that makes you want to rut like mad, but battle got me going.

Put all of that together, and I was almost wishing that Hal, the pixie, was still around.

"Ew," I said to my reflection, calming down slightly.

I walked out of the room, grabbed Kayson by the wrist, and said, "Let's go get a drink."

"As you wish," he replied as we strutted past Peggy, whose eyebrows were fully up in surprise.

We walked to the portal room and I gave Kayson a look.

"Where to?" he asked.

"I don't care," I answered, "as long as it's not the nightclub we were at earlier." He reached out to enter coordinates into the portal, but I stopped him and added, "Also, make it someplace decent. Remember, I'm supposed to be reputable as Grayson."

He looked himself over and squinted at me. "Maybe I should change, then?"

Honestly, I preferred his look. Rough and rugged was more my style than clean and sharp, but I had to keep up with the play. If the press up here was anything like it was in the Badlands, the image of Evelyn Grayson sitting in a club with someone like Kayson would hit the tabloids by morning. Based on the fact that she was boning her limo driver, I had the feeling that she was careful about who she was seen with in public.

"Yeah," I said with a nod, "go clean up first, and thanks for the reminder."

He gave me a wink and we begrudgingly headed back toward the changing room.

"Back already?" asked Peggy.

"Miss Priss can't be seen in public with a guy who dresses like a biker," Kayson teased before pushing his way into the room.

"I don't understand," Peggy said to me.

I flopped down in the chair on the other side of the counter.

"This body belongs to some wealthy woman up here," I explained. "Evelyn Grayson."

"*That's* where I saw you," Peggy gushed. "You're the one who goes around helping everybody." She stopped and blinked. "I mean, I guess *she* was the one who did that."

"Right."

"No, seriously, you're...she's one of the people the paparazzi chases after from time to time. Not like a regular celebrity or anything, but every now and then she gets her name in the papers and on TV."

The orc had the look of someone who was starstruck. She obviously knew I *wasn't* really Grayson, but something told me she was mentally wrestling with that fact.

"Pegs," I said, snapping her out of it, "I'm not Grayson. I'm Eve, remember?"

She shook her head. "Right. Sorry. I've just never met someone famous before."

"And you still haven't," I pointed out. "You've just met her body."

"Yeah...sorry."

Something told me that Peggy wasn't going to be able to look at me the same way again, at least not when I was inhabiting Grayson. That was good and bad, though. It was good because it would serve as a reminder that I wasn't truly *me* to the rest of the world. Everything I did when presenting as the wealthy philanthropist, had to fit the part if I was to avoid unnecessary attention. It was bad because I wasn't much of an actor. The real me had a tendency of being more like Kayson. I wasn't prim and proper, and I was damn happy about that.

On the plus side, I now had access to someone who seemed to actually give a shit about celebrities, even minor ones like Grayson.

I needed to use that.

"Pegs," I started, but was interrupted when Kayson stepped out of the changing room.

Both Peggy and I caught our breath at the sight of him.

He had shaved, combed his hair, and was wearing a suit that looked like it belonged on a wealthy businessman. To say he looked gorgeous was underestimating the point by a mile. He looked so condom-worthy that I would have forgone the condom. It's not like this was really my body anyway.

"Uh," was all Peggy could say as Kayson stepped over and gave us a confused look.

"Why are you guys looking at me like that?" he asked, seeming to be genuinely baffled. "Do I look stupid or something?"

"Not at all," I replied, shocked. "You look pretty damn amazing, in fact. Doesn't he, Pegs?"

Peggy's eyes were red. "I'd play Touch the Orc with him," she hummed.

"No, thanks," Kayson said, taking a quick step back. "I remember the first...and *last* time we did that. Couldn't walk for a week." He then leaned toward me and added, "Those tusks aren't just for decoration, let me tell ya."

Okay, so that knocked my horny points down a couple notches.

"Orcy-orcy porky-porky," Peggy moaned.

Kayson began pushing me back toward the portal room.

"We should go," he said, looking concerned for the first time since I'd met him. "Seriously, like now!"

CHAPTER 31

*T*o be safe, we went back to Grayson's office. The windows were still smoked, so nobody could see that we had arrived.

"Stay here," I said, motioning Kayson to hang back as I checked the door.

The main floor was empty, indicating that everyone had gone home for the evening. I waved at Kayson and he followed me down the hallway and out to the elevator.

"*Rainey,*" I called through the connector, "*I don't suppose you're near the office, are you?*"

"*I'm just now turning in, actually,*" she replied.

That was awfully convenient.

We took the elevator down and found the Rolls pulling up as we stepped out.

"Nice," Kayson said, grabbing the door for me as Rainey opened and then closed her own door. "Looks like Grayson definitely lived the good life."

"So it seems," I agreed as he closed me in and began walking to the other side.

"Who's the muffin?" Rainey giggled, looking in the rearview mirror at me.

"Kayson," I replied, "and shut up."

She giggled again, but gained her composure as soon as Kayson took a seat and shut the door.

"Where to, ma'am?" Rainey asked.

I glanced over at Kayson with a raised eyebrow.

"Take us to the Ritz," he said. "We're going to WP24."

"Excellent choice, sir," Rainey replied while backing up. *"They've got great food, and Grayson goes there often."*

"Good," I replied, trying to act like everything was normal. *"This is just a business thing."*

I don't know why I said it, especially since that was complete bullshit. I guess I felt strange about the entire ordeal. The last thing I needed was to have to deal with "knowing eyes" and all that crap. I was more of a fuck'em and leave'em type. Obviously, that wasn't going to work out being that Kayson and I were effectively peers in the PPD, but I had the feeling he was a no-strings kind of guy anyway. Rope? Maybe, but no strings.

"Uh huh," she replied.

"Shut up."

The buildings were lit up, reminding me of the other night when I'd escaped up here. I certainly had no desire for a repeat crash, and I definitely wasn't interested in running into anyone from Varaz, Mathen, or Tross. As long as I played the part of Evelyn Grayson, fooling any would-be pursuers would be a snap. The crashing part, I had no control over.

"Listen," Kayson said, giving me a quick look, "Q's a

dick and all that, has been since the first day I met him, but you get used to him."

"Seems you have a love/hate relationship with the guy," I noted.

"Love's a little much," he argued. "Let's just say that he's decent at what he does."

"Planning?"

"Yeah."

"But you *hate* planning."

"Not exactly," he replied, a look of mischief on his face. "Let's say that I love messing with his head. He's such a douche at times, and I know that when I pick on him and grumble at his plans and ideas, it riles him up. Call me passive-aggressive, I guess."

"Yeah. Well, if he keeps playing the game of shitting on the team for his own personal gain, I promise you I'll whoop his ass."

Kayson shrugged. "Can't say I blame you. I've done it more than once over the last few months."

We pulled up alongside a large building and Kayson played the role of gentleman again, jumping from his side of the car to open my door. This was definitely odd, knowing how he acted normally.

"*Have fun, Eve,*" Rainey said through the connection.

"*Shut up.*"

I got out and walked through the main entrance, and was immediately greeted by a number of people who were wishing me well after my ordeal. A few cameras came out and pictures were taken. Kayson handled it like he'd been on dates such as this many times.

"Done this before?" I whispered.

"All the time," he replied. "It gets boring hanging out at the GH Station every weekend, you know? I mean, unless you're Q, I guess."

"He doesn't really do that, right?"

The hotel staff rushed over to help clear the way so that we could get to the elevators. The woman I assumed was the manager, gave me an apologetic nod as we stepped into the lift and hit 24.

It opened to reveal a nice restaurant with interesting lighting. The maitre d' rushed over, looking anxious.

"Miss Grayson," he said, his face flushing, "it is wonderful to see that you are feeling better. I was so distraught when I'd heard what had happened."

"Thank you," I replied. "I'm sorry, though, but I have lost my memories. The doctors say that they will probably return, but it could be months."

He stood back with a look of shock. "How dreadful! Well, you don't worry one bit. We will take care of you as we always have, of that you can be sure."

The man pranced ahead of us until we got to a table that was near the back. It was somewhat secluded, which was fine with me. Kayson and I could simply chat via the connector, if needed, but I much preferred not using the technology. It still felt strange to me. Of course, if I worked to embrace it, maybe that would stop being the case eventually.

"Seems you're not as popular as me," I teased Kayson, after the maitre'd left to fetch us a waiter. "I'm guessing the ladies you bed down know better than to introduce you around?"

"Better for everyone that way," he replied. "I keep my privacy. They get laid. Win-win."

I sniffed at the comment. "You truly are sure of yourself, aren't you?"

"Supremely," he replied, and he was serious.

"This should be an interesting night, then."

"Again, supremely."

That time he grinned.

CHAPTER 32

*B*y the time we returned back to the Grayson residence, the majority of the staff had gone off to bed. Rainey had been wise to keep her mouth shut during the ride home, other than to announce, "Miss Paget has been told of our impending arrival."

The courtyard was quiet, except for Annette, who opened the door as soon as we pulled up.

"Good night, Rainey," I said, before stepping out.

"Good night, ma'am," replied Rainey just as Annette said, "Welcome home, ma'am."

"Annette," I said with a nod, "I have company for the rest of the evening. Please see to it that we aren't interrupted."

Kayson climbed out of the car behind me.

Annette blinked at him a couple of times and then looked back at me.

"*Well done, ma'am,*" she messaged through the connector.

I merely smiled and shook my head. He *was* a looker,

but I still wasn't sure if his beauty was only skin deep or not.

We headed upstairs and into my room, motioning for Cruze to go hide under the bed or something. I would have suggested the chair instead, but seeing as how Evelyn Grayson had a room specifically set aside for what I was about to do, I figured Cruze would have felt safer under the bed.

Instead of taking a hint, though, he waited until we were both in the room.

"That thing yours?" Kayson asked, looking somewhat twitchy as he pointed at Cruze.

"Grayson's," I replied. "Sort of."

Cruze had been prancing his way over toward us, when suddenly he stopped and stared up at Kayson. An instant later, the hairs on his back stood straight up and he hissed. Kayson growled in return.

"Oh, come on," I said, putting myself between the two of them. "I get it, I get it. You're a dog and he's a cat, but this is just ridiculous."

"He's not *just* a dog," Cruze shot back. "He's a hellwolf."

Kayson took a step back, looking shocked.

"Holy fuck potatoes," he said, staring at Cruze. "Your cat talks?"

I gave him a funny look. "No, my cat does not talk."

Kayson turned toward me, his face full of horror.

I giggled at that. Kayson frowned.

"Har har har," he said. "Seriously, though, you *did* hear that litter box user say something, right?"

"Go mark a tree, asshole," Cruze grumbled in response.

"See? He did it again!"

Honestly, for Kayson to be this freaked out about Cruze's ability to speak was pretty funny. It also made me wonder just how much of his brain was fully functional. At least he was pretty.

I decided to introduce them formally. "Cruze, this is Kayson. Kayson, this is Cruze."

"Hey," Kayson said with a slight wave.

"Sup?" replied Cruze. Then, his eyes snapped open and he glanced back and forth between us. "Hey, wait a second here. He's a hellwolf and you…" He brought his paw to his mouth. "Holy shit, Eve. *You're* the hellion who killed Willow?"

In the blink of an eye, I had Cruze pinned against a wall, dagger in hand.

"What have you heard, cat?" I growled.

"Chill, chill," he rasped. "I'm *not* just a lowly house cat, remember? I can get out and move around the town. I hear things. Lots of things."

"Which means you can say things, too."

Cruze frowned in a cat kind of way. "Why would I want to do that? What good would turning you in do for me? I'm trying to stay under the radar, too, remember?"

I held him in place for a few more seconds before taking my hand away. He landed on his feet and moved off to a safe distance.

"How did you hear about me?"

"Us," corrected Kayson.

"Yeah, I mean us," I amended. "How did you hear about us?"

Cruze studied the area for a few seconds, no doubt

hunting for a way out in case I decided to shave him or something.

"I hang out with a couple of people," he admitted. "Lower in the crime chain. Nice enough, if a little slow. One of them was flapping his gums about what happened at the nightclub down at the Crest."

"Go on," I pushed.

"Said that he witnessed the entire thing," continued Cruze. "One of those 'A hellwolf and a hellion walked in to a bar' kind of stories, just without a humorous punchline." He shook his head, sadly. "I can't believe you took Willow from us." There was a long sigh. "She will be missed."

By now, Kayson and I were glancing at each other. We said nothing, but nothing really needed to be said. We both knew the drill here.

"I don't suppose your informant would be a pixie by the name of Hal, would it?" Kayson ventured.

Cruze appeared taken aback by Kayson's question. "You know him?"

"Ugh," I said. "So much for Hal keeping his mouth shut."

"At least now I know why people shove him up their asses."

"Happens to him a lot," Cruze stated. "Truth be told, I think he's into it...in a manner of speaking."

The thought of that, and the fact that we had a loudmouth pixie running around telling people a hellion and a hellwolf had wasted Willow, had basically killed my desire for getting busy with Kayson.

I wasn't the type who could channel anger into sex.

That's when I remembered all the stuff that Grayson had in that naughty room of hers. Oddly enough, I felt a tingle go up my spine as I studied Kayson.

"What?" he said, squinting. "You're giving me a look that says I've been a bad boy."

So much for a potential resurgence in interest.

"Ew," was all I'd managed to say.

He clearly got the point because his face fell slightly. The fact that he realized it was a bit of a turn on. Damn it. Living in this body was going to take some getting used to, that was for certain.

"*Are you there?*" came the call of Q, sticking the proverbial nail in the coffin. "*We're being called in.*"

Kayson sighed, obviously having gotten the message, too. Something told me that his sigh also contained a fair bit of relief, though. It was clear that neither of us were ready for a round of, as Peggy had put it, orcy-orcy porky-porky.

"*We'll be there shortly,*" I answered, and then cut him off.

I wasn't in the mood to speak with Q.

"Back to the limo?" asked Kayson.

"No, just go from here. It's still pretty early. Hopefully, we'll be back in time to not make anything seem odd."

He nodded and tapped his tattoo, disappearing immediately.

I turned toward Cruze. "Sorry I gave you shit."

"Listen, I…" he started, but then paused and blinked a few times. "You're…what?"

"Truth is, I could use your ear in the underground here. If you have contacts, even that idiot Hal, that would be incredibly helpful to me."

"Yeah?"

"Yeah."

"Well," he said, stretching and dragging himself with his claws, "I suppose I could do that, especially if there was the promise of some catnip in my future."

That brought a grin to my face.

"I'll tell Annette."

"Sweet."

With that, I flipped over my wrist, tapped on my tattoo, and blinked off to headquarters.

CHAPTER 33

The hair on the back of Moloch's neck stood on end as he stared at them.

Andras had assigned Saffron and Hender to work with him in finding the girl from Sinister House. Both of them were assassins. Saffron represented House Mathen, and Hender was there from House Tross. Technically, they were on the same level as Moloch, but he was still considered the leader of the hunt. That didn't mean they'd listen to him by default, though, which meant he had to flex his muscles a bit.

They stood in the portal room at House Varaz, waiting for the technician to finish adjustments. Going through the Forbidden Loch had given the hellions a way topside without notifying the authorities, though it was risky in its own way. Using the portals was a different matter entirely.

Getting back to the Badlands required Moloch to traverse the Loch again. It was easier on the way back up than it was going down, but he still preferred to avoid it completely.

"How much longer is this going to take?" Moloch asked the technician, who seemed to be frantically working on his datapad. "Every minute is a minute wasted."

"Just another couple of minutes, sir," the man replied, upping his pace even more.

Moloch sighed and studied his new assassins.

Saffron was a rugged woman. She was muscular, built as though she had spent a lot of time lifting weights. Her hair was pulled back tight, revealing a number of scars on her face. Either she wasn't great at fighting or she constantly battled people who were a step better than her. If the latter, that would support Moloch's efforts; if the former, she would be dead by the end of the day.

Hender was the antithesis of Saffron. He was lean and somewhat short, coming up to Saffron's shoulder. To be fair, she was a few inches taller than Moloch. There was something shifty about Hender as well. His dark hair hung in wisps that seemed intent on slightly shading the man's eyes. When Moloch was able to actually see those eyes, though, they told a story of a man who had no soul. His was the kind who loved to kill. No purpose necessary.

Moloch was definitely going to have to keep the upper hand here.

"Experience?" he asked, looking at Saffron.

She snapped to attention. "Thirteen years in the Guard of House Mathen. Twenty-three confirmed kills, random Houses. Multiple hunting expeditions during the Hellwolf Wars, though no confirmed kills. Honors include—"

"Enough," Moloch interrupted, not looking for a complete rundown on her entire resume. Her response to his command was all he really needed to know. He turned toward Hender. "You?"

"I have no need to detail my accomplishments to a Varaz assassin," Hender said, his voice dripping with venom. "I'm here to kill a member of House Sinister for the glory of House Tross. Nothing more."

Moloch stared the man down. "Let's get something straight, Hender. You report to me during this mission, as specified by Task Force Leader Andras. You will not deviate from my plans, and you will not do anything to jeopardize anyone on my team simply so you can attain personal glory. Do we understand each other?"

Hender didn't reply. He merely held Moloch's gaze.

Moloch decided he was going to have to watch his back around that one.

"I've completed the changes, sir," the technician announced, breaking the tension. "It will send you to the location requested, and it won't be registered with the main network."

"Meaning nobody will know that we left?" Moloch asked.

"Well, I'll know, sir," the technician replied. "And Andras, of course. Plus there are a few other technicians who saw you—"

"I'm speaking about the Paranormal Police Department, you dullard," Moloch sneered.

The technician winced. "Not on this jump, sir. It's a one-time scramble. Difficult to do. It will show that someone has jumped from a location in the Badlands, but it won't detail who it was, where they jumped from, or where they're going."

Moloch nodded and motioned for the others to step on the platform. As soon as they were on, he joined them and waited for the transport to take place.

A few moments later, they arrived in an abandoned warehouse. It was dank and somewhat humid, which made Moloch feel at home.

Craff was all smiles as the three approached him. That smile fell almost instantly.

"They're not from Varaz," he stated.

"Your powers of observation are unmatched, Craff," Moloch stated. "This is Saffron of House Mathen, and that is Hender of House Tross."

There were no handshakes or even nods, just cold stares.

"Moving along," Moloch said, waving his hand in front of Craff's eyes. "What have you learned here."

Craff's smile returned, though it wasn't as wide.

"Over here," he said, walking toward the back wall. "I'll show you."

They passed a number of metal boxes and a few barrels, making Moloch curious about what this place had once been. There was a scent of soured malt in the air, but seeing that the place looked to have been abandoned for a long time, Moloch wasn't sure if that really provided him any useful clues. As he walked by one of the barrels, he noticed the name "Chestcroft Beer" on the side. That explained the smell and the barrels, anyway.

But Moloch's sense of curiosity was completely washed away when he turned the corner behind Craff.

Taped to a pole that connected from the floor to the ceiling was a pixie. His eyes were darting all over the place, and it was clear that he'd been struggling something fierce to get away.

"What have we here?" asked Moloch, relishing in the thought of torturing one of these little beasts. "A snack?"

"What?" blurted the pixie.

"Uh…maybe?" Craff said, frowning. "Before that, though, I was sneaking through the underground areas, looking for any information I could in order to find the bitch." That was the name they'd settled on for the Sinister House prey they were after. "I happened to hear this little asshole talking to a few people, and he mentioned a hellion."

Moloch's eyes shifted back to the pixie.

"Oh, shit," the pixie said. "I know that look. I don't like that look."

"You've heard something about a hellion in the area?" Moloch asked, his voice cold.

"I can't really talk about it, you shit corn," the pixie replied.

"Shit corn?"

"Uh…Mr. Shit Corn?"

Moloch reached out with lightning speed and punched the pixie right in the face.

Blood spurted from the little thing's nose and he yelped.

"Ow! Fuck, fuck!" He started spitting blood. "What the fuck, man? No reason for hitting me for being polite!"

"Polite?" countered Moloch. "You just called me Mr. Shit Corn."

"Exactly my point!"

"And you call that being polite?"

Saffron stepped forward. "Sir, it is the way of the pixies to use vulgarity when showing respect."

Moloch was baffled by that statement.

"The overgrown cock puppet is right," the pixie grunted, "Mr. Nice Guy."

Saffron looked pleased at being referred to as an overgrown cock puppet, but—based on new information —the Mr. Nice Guy bit made Moloch feel as though he'd just been insulted.

Just in case, he punched the pixie again.

After a few moments of blood spitting and groaning, Moloch stepped back and said, "You will refer to me as 'sir,' is that clear?"

"Yeah, yeah, yeah," the pixie rasped. "Whatever you say, guy...erm, sir. Just quit fucking plucking me in the face, will ya?"

Moloch crossed his arms. "You will tell us everything you know about the hellion or you will be tortured in ways that will make you beg that we were merely plucking you."

"You *did* say 'plucking me,' right?"

Moloch sighed.

"Hey, wait," the pixie said suddenly, his eyes going wide. "You guys are going to shove me up your asses, aren't you?"

As one, Moloch, Craff, and Saffron barked "No!" at the exact moment Hender cooed "Yes."

They all looked at Hender. He pulled at his collar for a moment. "I mean, no."

Moloch thought certain he'd heard the pixie mumble the word "damn."

"The hellion," he said in a strong voice, uncrossing his arms and extending his hand toward the pixie, his fingers set for a mean pluck, "where is she?"

"I don't know," replied the pixie, "but I'm pretty sure I know where she'll be soon."

"Where?"

"She's going after Macy Bale."

"Who?"

"Crime boss up here," replied the pixie. "Mean as hell. Loves shoving pixies up…uh…" The pixie paused. "Never mind. She's just really mean."

"Good," Moloch stated, lowering his hand. "Craff, prepare a stick that we can tape our new friend to so that he can lead us to this Macy Bale person."

"Aw man, come on," the pixie complained. "You don't have to do that. I'll never live it down, if you do."

"Live what down?" Moloch questioned.

"Being a fucking pixie stick, Mr. Nice Guy…erm…sir!"

Another pluck occurred moments later.

CHAPTER 34

Q seemed perplexed by Kayson's outfit. Obviously, the hellwolf had never taken the vampire out to dinner.

"Kayson," said Simone, sounding a bit sultry, "I've never seen you dressed up before. You look…delicious."

"What, this old thing?" Kayson replied, flopping back in his chair. "I throw it on every now and then."

"Yes, well…it's…very—"

"All right, all right," Leighton chimed in, before things got out of hand, "let's get to the task at hand here."

"I was," Simone countered.

"I'm talking about our mission, Simone," Leighton stated. There was a pause, before Leighton continued. "We did a bit of research on Macy Bale, and it does appear that she's connected to the larger threat in a very strong way."

"May I ask how, sir?" Q asked.

"It's not relevant to your job," Abner answered.

"True," agreed Leighton. "It's on a need-to-know basis, and none of you need to know."

"Then why are you telling us about it?" I questioned. "Seems like a stupid thing to do, if you don't want us to be curious about it."

I knew I was doing it again, but it bugged the hell out of me when someone went fishing with people. I'm not talking trolling here. I'm talking fishing. Where trolling is saying things that cause people to argue with you simply because you're having fun winding them up, fishing is what people did when they wanted you to respond in some way but they didn't want to just come right out and ask whatever it was they wanted. For example, when I was younger, my mother used to say things like, "I wish someone would take out the trash" or "I wonder what will happen when we run out of clean dishes." Just tell me to take out the fucking trash, mom!

Sorry.

Anyway, the point is that if Leighton didn't want us to ask questions about Macy Bale, he should have just told us what to do and have been done with it. But, no, that's not what happened. He intimated that she was connected with some larger picture, which would obviously elicit a curious response. He then pointed out that it was something we didn't need to know about.

He was fishing.

Fucker.

"Let's move along, shall we?" Simone said as the tension picked up again.

It was clear that I was a thorn they weren't used to in this room. Kayson was similar to me in many respects, but he didn't seem to care enough about anything to put up a huge fight. He was a "meh" kind of guy.

And Q was...well...Q.

"Indeed," Leighton said a few moments later, "let's move along. You are to head down to the Department of Building and Safety. That's where Macy Bale has her headquarters. It will be through a door that's behind a null zone and a hidden zone, so you'll have to find it on your own."

"And do be careful, Kayson," Simone purred. "I would sure hate for that suit to get tarnished in any way."

Leighton grunted and then shut down the connection.

"Seems like you have an admirer," I noted to Kayson as we headed out of the theater a couple seconds later. I gave him another once-over. "Can't say I blame her."

Q was ahead of us, but he stopped at the theater doors and looked back at us. His eyes were narrowed as he was clearly trying to suss out some puzzle that had instantly plagued him.

"Yes?" I asked, finally.

"Did you two have sex?"

I jolted slightly at that question.

"That's none of your business, Q."

"It most certainly is my business," he replied. "We are a team here."

"Uh..." I started and then gave him a confused look and tried again. "Are you saying that in order for me and Kayson to have sex, you need to be there, too?"

"Yeah, dude," Kayson laughed. "You want to film it or something?" He then gave me a quick glance. "I'm up for that, if you are, by the way."

"That is *n...not* what I meant," Q stammered. "In fact, that is really disturbing."

"Tell me about it," I agreed.

He looked briefly offended by my statement, but continued on. "What I'm saying is that the rules are very clear about interpersonal relationships between officers in the Black Ops Paranormal Police Department. It was in the manual, which both of you should have read cover to cover."

Kayson and I began studying our feet.

"You *still* haven't read it in full?" Q nearly shrieked. "I can *almost* understand why Eve hasn't read it, seeing that she's still very new, but you have no excuse at all, Kayson."

"Yeah, I do," Kayson argued, holding up a finger. "It's boring as shit. It's all rules and regulations, man. There's no action or drama, and it's sure as balls ain't funny at all."

Q just glared at him for a moment, before rolling his eyes and spinning to push his way out of the theater room.

"Unbelievable," he hissed, heading for his office. "You two are not to have relations, is that clear?"

"Nope," I replied.

"Not even slightly," stated Kayson.

Q stopped again.

"But it's against the rules!" His hands were up in the air and his face was scrunched in frustration.

"I get that, ya fanged dick," Kayson yelled back, "but *you're* the one who wrote those rules. They're not officially sanctioned or anything. You're just a little vampire who wants to run a fiefdom that has no sex, no eating after 8 p.m. no breaking of any rules, and no fucking fun at all."

They were both standing toe-to-toe with faces full of rage.

"No eating after 8 p.m.?" I ventured, after a few moments. "What's that all about?"

"Helps avoid acid reflux and offers many other health benefits," Q replied, keeping his eyes glued to Kayson's. "You would know that if you'd read the manual."

"Right," I said. "Well, sorry, but I'm with Kayson on this one. First off, not eating after 8 p.m. is going to be really tough, especially when we're out killing people and such in the wee hours of the morning."

"But—"

"Second," I went on without letting him get a word in edgewise, "breaking rules is only necessary when the rules are stupid, and most rules that are written by people who don't actually engage in the majority of jobs they write rules for…are stupid rules."

"I engage just fine in—"

"And lastly, I will happily agree to the 'no sex' rule with you, but I can't make the same promise with other officers in our little group."

Q's mouth closed into a tight grimace.

"That's just rude," he said.

"Sorry, Q, but you're kind of a dick." I shrugged at him. "Besides, you're the one who wrote these rules, so it's not like you want to knock boots with any of us anyway." I then leaned in slightly. "By the way, even though Dr. Gillian isn't technically in Black Ops, she's still part of the support staff for the PPD, right?"

Q merely swallowed in response.

I smiled in return. "That's the problem with rules like this, Q. There's always a line, and that line gets grayer by the minute." Just as Q was about to reply, I waved at him, "I've got to change before killing Bale."

I could almost hear Kayson's grin and Q's frown when Kayson said, "I'll join you."

CHAPTER 35

Predator and prey is the way of life, but often times the prey is more worthy than the predator.

— GARRICK - HOUSE OF SINISTER

*K*ayson went in to change first. I stopped off to speak with Peggy.

"So?" she asked, clearly expecting me to lay out a full romance novel's worth of details about the tryst I'd had with Kayson. "How many different ways did you guys bone?"

Okay, so maybe an erotica novel's worth of details.

"We didn't," I replied with a grimace. "Had a decent dinner, where he was quite the gentleman, actually."

"Really?"

"Baffled me, too. It was nice, though. Was good to have an hour of relaxation and decent food." I waved my hand at her. "Anyway, we headed back to my place to get busy and things went downhill from there."

Peggy gave me a pouting face, which looked really weird on an orc. "He couldn't get it up, huh? That happened when he was with me, too. You have to do this thing with your tusk where…" She stopped and looked at me. "Forgot, you don't have tusks. I suppose you could use a finger, but it probably wouldn't reach as easily."

I held up my hand while trying to fight back the bile that was building up.

"First, ew. Secondly, we never even got our clothes off."

"Oh! Well, there's your problem." She laughed and patted my arm in a mentoring way. "You can't have sex with your clothes on, honey."

"Actually, you can…sort of." I took her hand off my arm. "Anyway, when we got back to my place, my cat told us that he'd heard from a pixie how a hellion and a hellwolf had killed Willow."

Her face dropped immediately. "You killed Willow?"

"Aren't you told about our missions?" I asked, confused.

She shook her head.

"Well, that's just fucked up. How are you supposed to provide us with the proper technology when you don't even know what we're going to be doing?"

"I've said the same thing a number of times," Peggy stated, "but Q says that everything is to be kept top secret. It's all 'need to know' and everything. His air quotes, not mine."

Honestly, the power plays crap that people like Q used were not only stupid, they hurt the ability of people to professionally perform their jobs. I could almost understand the need for hiding details from someone who was out and about all the time, but Peggy was effectively trapped in the theater. She wasn't galavanting around, spilling secrets.

"From now on," I said, giving her a sharp look, "you demand to know what you're outfitting us for. If you're not told, refuse to do it."

"I wish it were that easy," she mumbled.

"What do you mean?"

"I'm only here because I'm useful. If I refuse to do my duties at all, I'll be sent back down to the Badlands." She cleared her throat, looking nervous. A shaky orc was even stranger than a pouting one. "Orcs are hunted in the Badlands."

That was true.

Most people thought they were extinct. That little piece of propaganda was spread by the orcs, though. There weren't many of them, and they went out of their way to keep themselves hidden, but they still existed.

"All right," I said to Peggy, "I understand your situation, but for me, specifically, I want the best stuff you have to offer for the mission I'm on." I paused. "The bracers, for example. Amazing stuff. I can hold my blades without even the slightest tremble."

She perked up. "Sweet."

"Very," I agreed. "Anyway, we're off to kill Macy Bale. I don't know anything about her, aside from the fact that she's a mean bitch."

"No kidding," Peggy stated. "My boyfriend says she's pretty awful."

I furrowed my brow at her. "Boyfriend? You holding back on me, Pegs?"

Her face flushed slightly.

"We just met a couple of weeks ago," she replied, looking around. "I've been keeping it kind of quiet."

"Where'd you meet him?"

"Here."

"At the theater?"

"Yeah," she said. "He had tripped and fell through the hidden zone. Was terrified when he first saw me, but it turned out he was majorly in to cosplay, so…"

I was blinking at her, locked in confusion about how that could have happened.

"But there's a null zone and a hidden zone," I said. "Unless he's a supernatural, he should never have even gotten close to that area."

"He's a normal," she said, shrugging.

"That's…odd." I then just considered the differences between an orc and a human. "Plus, you'll crush him."

"He's pretty big for a human. Comes up to my breasts."

Her eyes fluttered with that admission.

"All right," I said, feeling that something was strange about all this. "Well, be careful, okay? It sounds a little too convenient to me."

She frowned, but nodded. "Okay, I will."

That's when Kayson came back out, dressed in his normal attire. He was still hot, but not in a GQ kind of way.

It was time for me to get outfitted.

CHAPTER 36

*K*ayson and I approached the portal room to find Q standing in our way.

"I know you two just want to rush in and kill everything in sight—"

"True," I agreed.

"Sounds about right," Kayson added with a nod.

Q took in a deep breath. "The problem with that plan is two-fold. First off, it's not a plan."

"Sure it is," I argued. "It's a simple plan. You even summed it up perfectly. We go in and kill everything in sight."

"She's right, Q," Kayson stated. "In fact, I'd say that's the best plan I've ever heard you come up with...ever."

"Then there's the *second* issue," Q pressed on, proving that vampires can get red in the face. I suppose it was more of a pinkish hue, but for a vampire that was saying something. "Since you two idiots killed Willow, Macy Bale is certainly going to have heightened her security."

I wasn't sure why he'd considered that an issue. While

I couldn't speak for Kayson, it was never my intent to kill everything in sight by running straight at them. My plan involved a bit more stealth and finesse.

"Out of curiosity," I said, "are vampires and hellwolves taught the proper ways to fight against overwhelming odds?"

"Maybe," answered Kayson. "I mean, it's not like I had much of a chance to learn the ways of my people."

"True. Q?"

"We are each taught how to handle ourselves."

"Phrasing," mumbled Kayson.

I sniffed and cracked a grin. "I'm sure you are, Q, but what about actual attack tactics?"

He shifted somewhat uncomfortably, revealing that he had zero training in such things. That was both good and bad. It was good because his thinking on the subject could be molded without a lot of kickback. It was bad because it meant that he'd already planned something for us that would have likely failed.

Honestly, I was amazed these two stayed alive for as long as they had.

"What *was* your plan, exactly?" I asked.

"Not this again," Kayson complained. "Guess I'll go grab more popcorn."

I grabbed his arm. "No, stay."

He gave me a look. "Just because I'm a hellwolf doesn't mean I follow commands. I'm going to get popcorn."

I spun on him and pointed firmly at the chair near the wall. "Sit and stay, and I fucking mean it."

Kayson's face was almost as filled with shock as Q's,

but he walked over and sat on the chair. I chose the one next to him and then looked up at Q.

"So?"

"Uh…" Q started, but was clearly still amazed at my outburst, and at the fact that Kayson had obeyed me.

Maybe I *could* use some of Grayson's whips…ew.

"Let's go, Q," I commanded, motioning my hand for him to continue, "we haven't got all night."

He snapped himself back to business and started in. "My plan was to move in at three separate points, taking down the guards on the outer edges until we were able to break into the main section and kill Macy Bale."

"So a direct attack?"

"Yes."

"I noticed you said 'we' in that plan," noted Kayson. "Are you actually planning to fight for once?"

"Well, no. I was just including myself because I came up with the plan."

I brought my hand to my face and rubbed my forehead for a moment.

"So, let me get this straight," I began. "You expected me and Kayson to go on opposite sides of the building…or whatever the hell it is we're trying to breach…and fight against a bunch of highly-trained guards in one-on-one fashion until we get inside?" I saw Q was about to speak, but I held up a finger to silence him. "Then, we're going to fight even more guards—ones who will likely be better equipped than the ones outside, by the way—before finally getting to the inner circle of Macy Bale. And *if* we make it that far, and aren't too damn exhausted, we're to take out her most elite guards and then finally kill her as well." I leaned back and crossed my arms. "Sound about right?"

Q shuffled again. "When you say it out loud, it's not—"

"Not good at all, Q," I finished for him.

I knew I was being harsh on him, but this was not a plan worthy of success. If anything, we were looking at *maybe* surviving the first wave.

"Fine," he huffed. "What do *you* suggest, then?"

I told them.

CHAPTER 37

"*T*hat's her," Hal said as Moloch looked on. "I don't see the hellwolf, though."

Moloch had taken his team to the location that the pixie had suggested. It wasn't known if Evangeline from House Sinister was ever going to arrive, but Moloch had to take every opportunity he could find. Plus, he'd threatened serious pain against the pixie if he'd turned out to be wrong. So, either way, it would be a win.

Ultimately, he was pleased that she'd arrived. Her death was paramount.

There were two buildings that overlooked a shared courtyard. Both buildings were brown with dark windows and there was a shared lobby connecting them. Moloch had no intention of using that lobby, and he had the feeling that Evangeline wouldn't either...on her way out, anyway.

He looked down to watch as she walked up the left set of stairs as if she'd owned the place.

"Shouldn't we kill her now?" asked Craff.

Moloch had considered it, but he'd spent many years in the Varaz Guard, and so he'd learned patience. There were times when one acted with haste, but there were also times when one sat back and simply let events unfold.

"No," he decided. "Let's let her do her mission. If she fails, we get what we want; if she succeeds, fatigue will put her at a disadvantage."

"There is no honor in that," argued Saffron. "Her blood should be on our hands."

"No," Hender said, coming to Moloch's defense. "Our mission is to ensure that she dies. The last thing we need is to bring unneeded attention to ourselves."

"Precisely," Moloch said, giving a nod to Hender. "We wait."

"Uh…" Hal chimed in. "Sorry to interrupt and all, but seeing as how I've delivered on my promise, can I go?"

Moloch wanted to just kill the wretched little creature, but he'd made an agreement.

"Free the pixie," he instructed Craff, after first reaching out one last time to pluck the little creature.

CHAPTER 38

Sometimes, the best course of action is the direct course of action.

— GARRICK - HOUSE OF SINISTER

J was sure that Garrick would have challenged my thinking, but I saw no other real option. We'd already established that fighting all these guards with just me and Kayson was a losing proposition. Now that I was face-to-face with three of the biggest men I'd ever seen, I had to agree with my original assessment of the situation. Kayson and I would have been slaughtered.

These were clearly werebears.

One or two of them wasn't necessarily a bad thing, but I spotted a good twenty of them outside alone.

I stopped at the front door.

"State your business," one of the guards grumbled.

"I'm here to speak with Macy Bale."

"Do you have an appointment?"

"No, but just tell her that the woman who killed Willow wants to talk with her."

The guard snarled. "*You're* the bitch who killed Willow?"

I merely held his gaze.

"You really fucked up Saturday nights for most of the guys on staff here, you know?" he stated, stepping menacingly forward. "Are you going to make up for what she used to do for us?"

"Yeah," said another guard, who stepped in closer as well.

It took everything I had to hold myself back from summoning my swords.

"I...uh..."

"Nobody combs down our fur like Willow did," a third guard moaned. "She was the best."

"Exactly," agreed the main guard, his red eyes boring into mine. "Also the best at filing our nails."

"And cleaning our ears," mentioned the second guard.

"Oh, well...uh..." I stammered, "I'm sure something could be—"

"But I'd give all that up for another of her signature handjobs," guard one sighed.

"Or two," said the second guard.

"Or three," agreed the third guard.

The look on my face must have said it all, because they all backed up a step, looking more than a little wary.

"Tell Macy Bale I'm here," I commanded the main guard with a hiss, "before I give each of you a fisty."

I meant a punch in the face, but it was clear they'd thought I meant something else.

Thankfully, Kayson hadn't been around to point out my poor choice of words.

The guard gave me one last look before putting his hand to his ear. There were a few mumbled words and a couple of nods. Finally, he turned and motioned the other two guards toward me.

"Frisk her."

They approached and I gave each of them a quick, stern look. "If I catch either of you feeling me up, it's going to be a painful night."

They were respectful, but thorough.

That was fine. It wasn't like I was stupid enough to carry any weaponry on my person. I mean, I *was*, but they were magically summoned weapons, so there was no way they'd be spotted.

"She's clean," they said to their commander.

"Doubtful," he snarked and then moved out of the way. "Go in and to the left. Her assistant will guide you from there." As I started to walk past, he roughly grabbed my arm. "Don't try anything funny, either, lady. You might be all tough when it comes to talking, but when it comes to fighting, we'll snap your skinny ass in two."

I glanced down at his hand and then back up into his eyes, smirking.

"Somehow," I admitted, "I don't doubt that."

He let go, and I pushed my way through the glass door.

"I'm assuming you saw that I made it in?" I called through the connector.

"Yes," replied Q. *"While you kept them busy, Kayson was*

able to scale the wall on the shadowed side. He's on the roof now."

"*Searching for a way in,*" Kayson informed us. "*There's a door, but I'm worried it might be armed.*"

"*I'll get into their systems and check,*" Q replied. "*Give me a few.*"

If nothing else, Q *was* good at dealing with computers and technology. That was a skill I'd never personally picked up, and something told me that Kayson wasn't well-versed in it either.

"*Keep me posted,*" I said as I approached a young fae who appeared more pleasant than the werebears I'd just left.

"Good evening," he said in a musical voice. "Miss Bale is waiting for you."

I nodded and followed him through a series of hallways that opened up into a conference room on the other side. There were multiple guards, even larger than the ones outside, and they all had weapons in hand. Not swords either.

They had guns.

Big ones.

"Stay here, please," the assistant said with a smile. "Miss Bale will be with you shortly."

I nodded as the assistant walked away, leaving me behind to stay with the looming beasts who appeared to have dire desires for me. Obviously, everyone had a thing for Willow. On some fronts, even *I* had to admit that it would have been nice to have learned exactly how good she was at doing...well...whatever she did. I definitely knew how good she was at being controlling, so I could only imagine what her deeper capabilities allowed.

"The door is not armed," Q said. *"Standard access."*

"Going in," Kayson replied. *"How far down?"*

"Second floor," Q answered. *"They're on the bottom floor, near the back room. You'll be heading over where they are so you can break through."*

"Got it."

"Hey, guys," I added, *"just a quick note that there are a shitload of werebears in here and none of them are very happy with me."*

"Are you all right?" asked Kayson.

"So far," I responded, *"but if things don't go well, I fear a severe case of hand-cramps is in my future."*

CHAPTER 39

*M*acy Bale sat behind a thick glass window, which was obviously there to protect her in the event that I was able to take down all these guards.

She either had been to this rodeo before or she expected more from me than was likely possible. Sure, I could mage and have the rare dual-wield, but there were quite a few werebears in here. But she was right not to take chances, assuming she thought anything like I did. The fact was that we were in a relatively enclosed space. That meant that I'd really only have to fight one bear at a time, and when one of them fell, the next one would be even easier to fight...or I could just run.

The sound of the door behind me clinked, signaling that it had been locked.

I looked up at Bale, finding the corner of her mouth had edged up slightly.

Seemed like we *did* think alike.

She was a vampire, which was not surprising seeing

that they had a tendency of being able to manage multiple races without too much fuss. Werebears and werewolves were a bit territorial, and they struggled to understand other cultures, at least when it came to a boss/employee relationship. They seemed to do okay with peers, and they were fine reporting to other races, but managing was an exercise is futility...and often murder.

"You have guts coming here," she said through a speaker system as she leaned back and crossed her arms, staring at me with obsidian eyes. "Honestly, I would have just had you killed in the courtyard, but I thought it'd be more fun to watch the spectacle."

"Hence, why you're hiding behind glass?" I asked, unable to control myself.

"I'm not a fool," she replied.

I glanced around at all the guards and their menacing faces.

"No arguing that," I rasped.

"So, you're here," said Bale, tilting her head, "which means you're either incredibly smart or incredibly stupid." She pushed her crimson hair away from her face. "What is it you wanted to say before I have you killed?"

"I'm hoping you're coming soon," I said to Kayson.

"Heh...I'm not even breathing heavy."

"Hilarious," I shot back. *"I'm about to be killed here, so cut the jokes and get your ass in gear!"*

"Oh, calm down," he replied. *"I'll be dropping in on her in about thirty seconds. Just setting the charges."*

I cleared my throat and gave Macy Bale a firm look, one that said I meant business.

"I want to take over Willow's spot," I said, which caused all the werebears to regard me in a somewhat different manner. "Not *everything* she does, mind you," I quickly amended. "I'm talking about the business side of things."

"And so you thought that shoving a sword through her neck would somehow endear you to me?"

"No," I replied, "but I have the feeling you are more interested in business than in friendship and feel-good moments."

"I'm not so sure I'd agree with that," Bale countered. "Willow's 'feel-good moments' were rather amazing."

That elicited a number of growls from the room. Not good growls, either.

"*Ten seconds,*" Kayson called out. "*Forgot I had to double wrap these damn things.*"

"You know what I think?" Bale asked. "I think you're just some wannabe hotshot, who accidentally got the better end of a fight. You then realized that you were going to be hunted, and so instead of spending the rest of your numbered days on the run, you decided to walk straight into the jaws of the shark and hope the shark wouldn't flinch."

"*We're at like twenty seconds, Kayson,*" I informed him.

"*I know, I know. The damn things won't trigger.*"

"*Did you shut off the secondary safety switch?*" asked Q. "*You always forget to do that.*"

"*Shit.*"

"The problem you have, my dear," continued Bale, "is that I'm one shark who *never* flinches."

"*Now!*"

The ceiling exploded, blowing a massive hole that sent debris straight down, carrying the falling body of Kayson with it. He landed on his feet, ready to attack.

Unfortunately, he'd landed in the office *next* to the one Macy Bale was occupying.

CHAPTER 40

J had my blades out before the dust settled. A few others had been shredded by glass in the explosion, and the two at my feet were struggling to get to their feet. Fortunately for me, those big dudes made for a great firewall.

My head was ringing from the explosion, but not as bad as everyone else's in the room. Seeing as I was the only person in the room who knew what was really going on, I'd thrown my hands to my ears and buried my face into the corner by the door the instant Kayson had yelled, "Now!" That gave me quite the edge over the rest of them.

"Wrong room, asshole!" I yelled through the connector, even though I knew Kayson was well aware of that fact. He turned to his right. *"She's on your left."*

"Shit."

He spun and started setting a charge on the wall that separated him from Bale.

Werebears were stumbling all over the place, looking

like they'd just been spun way too fast on a merry-go-round.

I could have killed each of them outright, but they weren't my target. Eventually, one or more of them probably would be, but that was for another time. Garrick had taught me a number of lessons in life, one of which being that you didn't just go about killing because you could. That thought reminded me of how Kayson and I had planned to kill everything in sight. Clearly, actions and words were two very different things.

Still, I had to immobilize them all.

"*Cover your ears,*" I commanded Kayson, who was still working away at the charge.

"*Why?*"

"*Just fucking do it!*"

He grunted and covered them, giving me a frustrated look.

I returned my blades and called power into my hands. Just when I felt there was enough energy to do the trick, I dropped powerfully to one knee, slamming my palms on the floor.

A blast of blue energy flew out in all directions from me, throwing bodies into the air while simultaneously releasing a loud "Whoompf!"

Unfortunately, I'd put a little *too* much power in that hit, which became obvious when Kayson hit the ceiling along with Macy Bale.

Everyone crashed back to the floor a second later, completely out. Not even a moan sounded.

"Oops," I whispered as I rushed over to make sure Kayson was okay.

I slapped him a few times, and then channeled a little healing energy into him.

His eyes snapped open and he shook the cobwebs out.

"What the fuck just happened?"

"Uh…you didn't cover your ears in time."

He squinted at me. "I think you're lying."

"Mayyyyybe," I replied at length as I dragged him to his feet. "I put a little too much juice in that magical blast."

"Ya think?" he said, refocusing on blowing a hole through the wall into Bale's room. "Might want to back up."

I did.

He triggered the explosion.

Interestingly, it was some kind of one-way thing. We felt a little of the shock, but it was barely enough to move me. The sound hadn't been very bad either.

Macy Bale, however, hadn't faired as well. Her body seemed to be okay. It no longer had a head attached to it.

"That's lovely," I said, spotting her head in one of the potted plants on the far side of the room.

"What's going on?" asked Q. *"All the guards are rushing into the building."*

Kayson and I looked at each other.

"Shit," we said in unison, rushing back into the original room he'd landed in.

I dropped and made a cradle for his foot. Obviously, he'd played this game before because he stepped right in and pushed off as I pushed up with all my might. He launched perfectly to the second floor and dropped to reach out a hand. I grabbed it and he pulled me up as if I weighed nothing.

Tingle.

We took off down the hallway, hitting the stairwell in a flash.

It was only a matter of time before the werebear guards figured out where we'd gone, so we ran with all our might, heading toward the roof.

"*Did you get Macy Bale?*" Q asked, sounding as frantic as we felt. Of course, his angst was more to do with the completion of the mission and not so much to do with our personal well-being. "*We must ass—*"

"We got her, dickhead," Kayson barked, interrupting him. "*We're okay, too, in case you were worried.*"

"*I'm asking because a number of the guards have rushed back outside and are clearly searching for you.*"

That was good, at least. It meant they weren't on our tail just yet. Still, it was only a matter of time.

I grabbed Kayson by the arm as we sped past floor number six.

"Hold up!"

He stopped, looking back at me.

"You have any more of those explosives?"

"Yeah, why?"

"Follow me."

I opened the door and took off through the maze of desks that made up whatever office space we had entered. If I was to make a guess, I'd have said it was some kind of accounting firm because it was seriously bland. Everything was brown, except the carpet, which was gray.

"Drab," Kayson noted, only a couple steps behind me. "What are we doing, anyway?"

In response, I asked, "I'm assuming you can time these

explosives?" just as we made it to the opposite stairwell door.

"No," Kayson replied, "but I can remotely detonate them. Why?"

"Good enough." I started pointing at the various concrete walls. "Put one there, there, and there."

"Why, why, and why?"

"Because we're going to blow this stairwell up, Kayson," I explained with a growl. "Duh!"

"I get that, *Evangeline*," he shot back. "But why the fuck are we doing that?"

"Diversion!"

"Oh...right."

Kayson started placing the charges where I'd told him to. I would have helped, but I'd never messed with those types of bombs before and I certainly had zero desire in becoming a statistic.

I heard a crashing sound and looked out the little glass portal into the office space we'd just crossed through. One of the werebears had opened the door on the other side.

On a whim, I rushed out and got partway across the office, acting like I hadn't seen him. Then, I stopped and yelled, "Oh, shit," and ran back the other way.

"Got 'em!" he yelled back into the stairwell on his side before I felt the heavy clomps of his massive boots heading my way.

The bait had been set.

"They're here," I called over to Kayson, taking two steps at a time. "Let's get the fuck out of here."

I thought I was fast, but Kayson took speed to an entirely new level. It was all I could do to keep up with him. We got up four levels before running out onto an open office floor. There were plenty of guards churning up the steps to make our mark and create that full diversion. I felt kind of bad about what we were going to do, but it felt a lot better than what those werebears would have done if they got their hands on us.

As soon as we were halfway across to the other side, I yelled for Kayson to blast the fuck out of the place.

The explosion was much louder than the ones before, and stronger too. They were so strong, in fact, that both Kayson and I were thrown to the floor.

"What the fuck?" I asked, pushing myself up and continuing the run. "Were those the same kind of charges?"

"Yeah," he answered. "I just forgot to set them to be directional. I was in kind of a rush, you know?"

"*What in the world is going on in there?*" Q chirped through the connector. "*The entire side of the building just blew up!*"

"*Kayson forgot to set the directionals on the charges,*" I answered. "*And, yes, we're still fine. Thanks for asking.*"

"*Dickhead,*" Kayson added.

With the guards destroyed on that side of the building, and the very strong likelihood that most of the attention would be focused there, we were able to get to the rooftop without too much worry of there being more werebears on our asses.

I pushed out into the night and came to a screeching halt.

Leaning against the wall across from the doorway was Moloch and three other hellions.

CHAPTER 41

The tiniest spark can build to engulf a massive forest, but a bomb gets the job done quicker.

— GARRICK - HOUSE OF SINISTER

My first thought was to blast the hell out of them, using up all the magical reserves I had in the tank. My second thought was that if I missed, both Kayson and I would be minced meat.

I had to put the House first.

"I thought I smelled something funny on the run up here," I said as Moloch pushed away from the wall, motioning for his pals to fan out. "It was the smell of sadness."

"And shit," amended Kayson. "Definitely smelled shit."

"Yes, agreed," I said, giving him a nod. "I noticed that, too."

Moloch's eyes were cold, which meant he wasn't going to fall for my razzing this time.

So I summoned my blades and stepped away from the door. Kayson stayed put, keeping himself halfway in the stairwell.

Was he planning to run?

I studied him for a moment and saw what was really happening.

He was shifting.

Kayson was going full hellwolf.

That both worried me and lifted my spirits a bit.

The howl that filled the air a few moments later was deafening, and certainly had to have reverberated down the stairwell as well. That would signal the werebears of our whereabouts.

Good.

All the hellions were frozen, fixated on what Kayson had just become.

To say he looked like a wolf would be understating things pretty heavily. I mean, he *did* look like a wolf, but he was one big fucking wolf. I'm talking shoulder high, massive teeth, glowing green eyes, and a tail that was wagging a little too happily.

"*Ready?*" he asked through the connector, jolting me from my stupor.

"*Uh...you can still talk?*"

"*Only through the connector,*" he replied.

"*That's...cool, I guess?*"

"*Thanks,*" he said, dropping on his butt and scratching his ear for a second. "*That itch has been bugging me for...*" He paused and sniffed the air. "*Werebears are coming up the stairs."*

That definitely put me back in business-mode.

"Good, we just need to keep these pricks busy long enough for them to arrive."

"Why would we want to do that, again?" he asked, giving me one of those looks that dogs get when they hear an interesting sound.

"Because the bears will fight the hellions and we can get the fuck out of there."

"Oooh! I like it."

With that, Kayson bolted toward the guy to the right of Moloch. He was one of the original hellions who had chased me when I'd escaped the Badlands. The other two hellions, ones I hadn't seen before, were basically falling over themselves to get away from the hellwolf.

That left me and Moloch to square off.

"I see you've picked up a doggie," he said as he jumped forward and sliced at me with his blade.

He was fast. Faster than I would have expected, in fact. There was no wavering in his swinging arc at all. It was smooth, straightforward, and deadly.

I caught the attack off the edge of my blade and sliced at his calf with my other.

Obviously, he was not used to dual-wield, because the hit struck perfectly. Unfortunately, that's when I learned that Moloch wasn't stupid. He was wearing protective clothing. The sign of a *true* assassin.

My blades weren't getting through those.

But it still caught him off guard enough that his face registered shock.

"Yeah, asshole," I said, moving back away from him.

"Every time your one blade comes in, I'll have a second one to slice you with. It's what makes a 'bitch' like me so damn difficult to deal with."

"Too bad for you that I have worn the proper attire, then, no?" he countered. "Plus, I have friends who can serve to ensure that your two blades simply won't be enough."

A roar and a growl stunned us both, but the scream that followed made me stumble backwards.

I glanced over to find that Kayson had chomped down so hard on the arm of the guy he'd been facing that blood was spilling everywhere. Obviously, that poor fucker hadn't had the same kind of clothing as Moloch.

With a massive shake of his head, Kayson flopped the guy around like he was a child's doll, finally releasing him with a launch over the edge of the building. He then turned to look at the other two hellions.

They both had their hands out in fear.

"That was terrifying," I pointed out. *"Do it again!"*

"That's the plan."

Too bad that was also when a bunch of werebears crashed through the stairwell door and started the process of turning.

"Shit," I hissed, stowing my blades and then giving the finger to Moloch. "Smell you later, asshole."

He sneered but clipped something on his belt to the roof and jumped up on to the ledge of the roof. The other two hellions followed suit. Honestly, I was kind of surprised they hadn't done that sooner.

"Good luck with your new friends," he said with a laugh.

"You mean you're not going to stick around to kill me yourself?" I asked. "Not that you could, but you know what I mean."

"It doesn't matter *how* you die, bitch," he replied, loosing his mirth. "It only matters *that* you die."

He jumped.

I turned toward Kayson, who was in the middle of a standoff with five very large, very angry werebears. But even they looked tentative about attacking a hellwolf. I couldn't say I blamed them, either. He was roughly the same size they were.

"Any suggestions?" Kayson asked.

"Aside from magic, the only thing I can think to do is stand our ground and fight."

Kayson nodded. *"Magic it is, then."*

"Shit."

CHAPTER 42

"*K*eep them occupied while I get everything set up," I commanded, doing my best to draw as much magic as possible into my hands. "*This isn't going to be easy, and if I fuck it up...we're dead.*"

"*What are you doing, exactly?*" Q asked, reminding me that he was still out there waiting for us. "*You've blown up part of the building, one person plummeted to their death, three people rapelled down about a minute ago, and now you're getting something else set up?*"

Being interrupted when trying to work with magic was not a fun proposition. Kayson was doing his best to keep the werebears occupied, mostly by growling at them. They were clearly mesmerized by the hellwolf.

Not that I could blame them.

He *was* pretty scary-looking.

"*We've got multiple werebears up here, Q,*" Kayson replied. "*I've gone full wolf and am keeping them at bay. Eve's hooking up magic to fight back.*"

"Ah," he said, and then added, *"Maybe you two idiots could just use your PPD tattoos and transport back to base?"*

Fuck.

No, wait…

"Wouldn't that be trackable from here?" I asked. *"I don't know who the big boss is, but I doubt it was Macy Bale. Whoever was pulling her strings has some pretty heavy money."*

"Your point?"

"Simply that he or she probably has eyes and ears all over the place."

"And scanners," agreed Kayson. *"She's right, Q. We tap the tattoo on this building and we might get traced."*

"Yes, but—"

I shut them both out and turned my attention back to my job.

One of the werebears turned toward me as my hands started to glow blue. That's when I realized that I should have been facing the other way while doing this.

Too late.

Kayson must have spotted it also, though, because he let out what I could only consider a war howl. It was incredibly loud and sounded like he'd just downed three burrito supremes from Taco Bell, including fire sauce.

It took everything I had to stay focused on what I was doing.

I opened the connection again, this time directly to Kayson.

"Remember that little spell I cast earlier?"

"The one that launched me head first into the ceiling?"

"That's the one."

"*Go on,*" he said, sounding more than a little concerned.

"*When I tell you to run, run,*" I stated, my concentration wavering.

"*Where?*"

"*Toward the wall on the other side. But here's the even more important part: when I tell you to stop, you stop immediately and jump like a motherfucker.*"

He looked over at me, green eyes glowing. "*You want me to jump off the building?*"

"*No!*" It was all I could do to keep focused. "*I want you to stop in place and jump straight up in the air.*"

"*May I ask why?*"

"*Run!*"

"*Aw shit crap fuck dick tits ass!*" he said, and took off.

The werebears seemed shocked to see him go, but their brains caught up with what was happening a second later and they took off after him.

I kept a steady stare at them, waiting for the timing to be perfect. Kayson was almost at the edge of the building. He couldn't go too far, but it had to be far enough or this wouldn't work and I'd be completely spent.

"*Now!*"

I dropped straight down, slamming my hand on the roof with everything I had. The energy flew out of my body like a tornado-sized sneeze, causing me to fall over the instant the magic blew out.

Luckily, I landed on my left side, which allowed me to see what happened next.

Kayson had stopped and jumped up, just as I'd

commanded him to. That allowed him to avoid the magic wave that spread across the building.

The werebears, however, weren't so lucky.

They flew up in the air also, and at roughly four times the height Kayson had been able to jump. The difference, though, was that their forward momentum was still in play, causing them to not only clear Kayson's body by a wide margin, but also sending them over the edge of the building in the process.

Kayson landed and ran over to the edge of the building, putting his paws up on the side and looked down.

The roars of falling werebears were silenced a moment later, after a resounding splat.

"*Nasty,*" said Kayson.

My response was to just pass out.

CHAPTER 43

I awoke to find Kayson hovering over me. At least I assumed it was him, since he was in wolf form. Thing was that he was now the size of a normal wolf.

"You can stop licking my face now," I groaned. *"I'm awake."*

"Sorry," he replied. *"Instinct."*

"It's an instinct to lick someone's face?"

"No...well, actually, kind of. But I mean when one of my pack is down, it's a way to rouse them."

"Ah." I pushed myself up to my elbow. *"You're a lot smaller than before."*

"I can control my size," he said. *"Perks of being a hellwolf."*

"You mean you can get bigger than you were before?"

"No, that's my full size," he replied. *"I can get smaller, though."*

"Obviously," I replied, motioning at him.

"This is just my normal size. Watch this."

At that, he sat down and his eyes glowed green as he

began to shrink. By the time he was done, he was about the size of a teacup poodle. Cute as hell, but completely useless. I imagined that even a pixie could whoop his ass without the need to resort to using dust.

"*Pretty fucking cool, right?*" he asked.

It was strange to hear a tiny dog cuss.

"*Uh, yeah. Not sure what use there is for being that size, but—*"

"*Are you shitting me? I'm fucking adorable like this. Major distraction.*" He pranced over and nuzzled my arm. "*Admit it, even you want to pick me up right now, don't you?*"

Damn it. I did.

I didn't tell him that, though. Instead, I focused on the rooftop again.

"*I'm surprised that more werebears haven't busted through the door to end us.*"

"*Q contacted me while you were out,*" he replied. "*Said that everyone was rushing out of the building since firetrucks were closing in. Also, said your hellion pals took off.*"

"*That's good.*"

My head was swimming. I needed to eat in order to get some strength back. Peggy had said she was going to work on something to help me maximize my magical efficiency. Until then, I was essentially a slobbering mass of exhaustion. The only things that gave me energy back were sleep and food.

"*Yeah, like that,*" Kayson said, turning his head into me. "*Right behind the ears. Aw yeah...it's like heaven.*"

Damn it.

I pushed him away.

"*I need food,*" I told him. "*Shift back to your normal size before I kick you off the building.*"

He turned and gave me those little puppy eyes.

"*It's not going to work, Kayson,*" I sniffed, even though it *was* working. "*I know who you really are, remember?*"

"*You're no fun,*" he said, his eyes doing that glowing thing again.

As soon as he was back to normal, he helped me to my feet and wrapped an arm around me so I wouldn't fall over.

He laughed. "You really are useless after using magic, aren't you?"

"After releasing that much power, yeah." I tried to stand on my own two feet, but it was no use. He had to be my crutch or I had to lie back down for another few minutes. "I really need some food."

"How about Italian? I know a little place right down the street. Brand new joint, so they're still trying hard."

"Don't care," I answered.

We moved over to the ledge on the opposite side of the roof. There was a thin cable connected to the wall. Obviously, this was how he'd scaled the building before.

"I don't have the energy to reppel, Kayson," I pointed out.

"I know," he said, sweeping me up in one arm and then deftly jumping over the side, sliding down the face of the building like it was nothing.

Again, tingle.

CHAPTER 44

The food was amazing. That they were open at this hour was even more amazing, especially with it being so empty.

I had angel hair pasta with some type of rose sauce, which seemed like tomato sauce and cream. The portion size was enormous, but I was already well over halfway through. The garlic bread was crispy and soaked with butter, which made chowing down easy.

"This is amazing," I said between ravenous bites.

"You sure you're not a werepig?" Kayson asked, his face slack at the amount of food I was shoveling in. "You've already had a slab of lasagna, you know?"

"Don't judge me," I shot back, giving him a look. "I told you that magic kills my energy."

"Yeah, but you didn't say that it made you eat like a buffalo."

I set my fork down long enough to give him the finger.

Another few minutes went by before the plate was licked clean and all the bread was gone.

Time for dessert.

I ordered a cannoli, despite the fact that Kayson was shaking his head at me in disapproval.

The moment the waiter set it in front of me and I reached for my fork was when the door to the restaurant burst open.

Standing there, sword drawn, was Moloch.

I growled, set my fork down, and pushed myself up from the table.

"I believe it's—" he started.

"Shut the fuck up," I interrupted him, sneering at his pompous face as I slowly walked in his direction. "You destroy my House, make me swim through the Forbidden Loch, force me to escape topside, and go out of your way to try to kill me at every turn. I can deal with that because it's the way of our people."

My hands flashed as my swords appeared on my back.

"But now, asshole, you went and broke a cardinal rule that's now going to cost you your life."

He raised an eyebrow in question.

"*Never* interrupt a woman who is about to eat dessert!"

CHAPTER 45

Honor is a fickle beast. It defines and governs our actions, be they good or foul; it builds our resolve when the will is weak; and it can raise an army that will follow us to the ends of the world.

But never forget that honor's purpose is to guide us in life, not in death.

— GARRICK - HOUSE OF SINISTER

We stood in the middle of the street staring down at each other. Moloch stood in front with his two hellion goons flanking him on either side. We'd moved outside of the restaurant to take care of business. I had no intention of bringing destruction to a restaurant with food so yummy.

"Going to use your magic again?" Moloch asked, as if noting it wasn't honorable.

"I'd be happy to shut down the magic, shit stain," I

replied, seeing his face twitch at being called a name. "Hell, I'll even duel you one-on-one and only use one blade."

He tilted his head at that.

"But you have to call off your goons as well."

Moloch flicked his hand in the air, signaling for them to back off.

They just stood there.

He turned to look at them. "Saffron and Hender, did you not see me flick my hands at you? That means for you to go away." They remained still. "Did you not hear? I'm fighting her one-on-one."

"Fuck you, Moloch," Hender replied in a smooth voice. "We are here to kill her, not to support your honor."

Saffron grabbed Hender's arm. "Wait a moment. What do we care if she kills him? If nothing else, it will tire her out."

Hender appeared to consider this for a moment.

"There's also the fact that I'll rip the fuck out of the both of you, if you interfere," noted Kayson, his eyes beginning to glow green.

A few moments later he had changed.

Nobody moved.

"He's all yours," Kayson said through the connector. *"Don't worry, though, I won't interfere. I know you guys take duels seriously in the hellion world. If he wins, he wins."*

"Fuck that," I shot back. *"If he starts winning, kill his sorry ass."*

"Ah...okay."

"One thing, though?" I added.

"Yes?"

"*You'd probably be more imposing if you weren't in teacup poodle mode.*"

"*Shit.*"

He grew to full size and growled, showing his huge fangs to make up for the fact that he had just made a fool of himself.

"*Better,*" I said as I slid my second blade back in its sheathing.

That just left me and Moloch to face each other down. I knew he was a solid fighter, I'd seen that his blade didn't waver when slicing. He was formidable. Was he as good as me? Doubtful, but seeing that I had essentially tied my own hand behind my back by promising not to use my second sword or any magic, it put us on even ground.

I never agreed to fight clean, though.

Moloch began circling to the left, signaling he was looking for an old-fashioned battle. He wanted this to be an epic event. One that would be spoken of through the ages. "Here's the man who solidified the finality of House Sinister."

I couldn't help but smile at that.

While I knew better than to underestimate anyone, I had no intention of losing this battle. Moloch was fighting for personal glory, I was fighting for Garrick and the House of Sinister.

He dove forward, piercing straight ahead with his sword. I sidestepped, fending off the attack with my blade while spinning away to regain the distance between us.

His eyes danced as he jumped in again, this time bringing his blade down in an angled-chopping motion that was clearly intended to cut through my shoulder.

I dropped down and brought my blade up, turning it slightly so that Moloch's attack would slide harmlessly away.

Then I punched out, connecting with his solar plexus. He grunted as I followed that with a slice to his leg.

Those damn pants protected him from the cut yet again.

I jumped back and held the sword out as he glared at me.

"So, let me get this straight," I said between breaths. "I give up the use of magic and my second blade, but you get to keep wearing clothes that are impervious to my attacks?"

"What would you have me do," he badgered, "strip?"

"No, don't do that," I said quickly. "It's one thing to die by being cut, but it's quite another to die from laughter."

The hellions giggled and Kayson did something that sounded like a mix between a bark, a growl, and a yawn.

"You'll die for that, bitch," hissed Moloch.

"Is that just the latest reason you're going to kill me, dipshit?" I goaded him, pushing any button I could. "I mean, it all started out with you killing me because you were trying to exact the Rite of Decimation."

"Well, yes, it is," Moloch replied, looking confused.

"You Varaz boys just aren't very bright, are you?" I said, laughing. I then glanced over at the other two hellions. "Honestly, you both *do* realize that you're tying your boats to a bunch of fucking idiots, right?"

They glanced at each other as Moloch unleashed a war cry and raced right at me, sword held high.

Now, I could have done the old wait-for-him-to-get-close-enough-and-then-drop-and-slice-his-gut-open move, but we all knew that wasn't going to work. He had on that damn armor.

So I did something he wouldn't expect.

I brought my blade up in a swift motion, releasing it at just the right moment so that it would launch directly at his open mouth. Then, I rolled out of the way and grabbed my second blade, just in case.

Fortunately, it wasn't needed.

My blade had hit home, stopping Moloch in his tracks for a moment before he fell straight forward onto his face, pushing the sword in even further.

A growl and a scream later, I spun to find Kayson on the chest of Hender, ripping out his throat. The hellion's hand released a small tube that was no doubt holding a poisoned dart.

Honor, indeed.

Saffron, seemingly the smartest of the bunch, was already hightailing it down the street, *away* from us all. She was no doubt going to go and report what had happened, telling the powers that be how I had destroyed their assassin with the help of a hellwolf.

More would be coming, but that was for another day.

For now, the asshole who had been the impetus for my arrival topside was dead.

CHAPTER 46

"So, you're in the clear, then?" asked Q. "No more worries about assassination attempts on your life?"

I shook my head at him. "The Houses aren't going to give up that easily, I'm afraid. They want me...no, they *need* me dead before the year's out. If they fail, I'll have them executed and then I'll take over all their Houses." I rolled my eyes and sadly smiled. "Shit, I could even claim the throne."

"Nice," Kayson said.

I refocused on Q. "Nobody down there wants that, though. There hasn't been a king or queen for a very long time, and that's how they like it. My survival is not in anyone's best interest in the land of the hellions."

Peggy walked over and put her hand on my shoulder. "I know how it feels to be alone with everyone wanting you dead."

"Yep," agreed Kayson.

We all looked at Q.

"Sorry," he said, "but we don't have such strange rules in my land. If you're wanted dead, they'll kill you, certainly, but there is no attempted genocide of a race or just a House. We don't even technically have Houses, though I suppose family names are close enough."

We all sat in silence for a few moments.

I'd spent a lot of my days worried about myself and what I was going through. I hadn't really taken the time to see that Kayson and Peggy *were* indeed in the same boat as me. I mean, I'd known that they were, of course, but I was just too wrapped up in myself to really care.

To be fair, I hadn't known either of them very well at the time.

As I stood there, I recognized that these people were my new family. They were the people who replaced the Guard. That was sad on many levels, especially since Garrick would have fired Q long ago, but it was also a good thing.

There *was* one element about all of this that scared me more than not surviving that year, though.

It was the knowledge that *I* was the new Garrick.

ruze hit the town for a bit, bored with just hanging around the house. It was a nice place and all, and it was definitely preferable than being caught in the real world...but sometimes the call of reality was just too tempting.

"...and then this crazy fucker starts plucking me with his big fat finger," said Hal, one of Cruze's many "friends."

Calling him an actual friend wasn't accurate. Sure, they hung out together now and then, but mostly Hal was there to give Cruze information. He was certain that Hal didn't know that, but seeing that the pixie was somewhat self-involved, as were most pixies, it was understandable.

"I mean, I can understand being shoved up someone's ass," Hal continued. "That's normal, you know?"

"Not really."

"But plucking a guy? Come on!"

"So who was it?"

"Some dude named Moloch," Hal replied. "Real nice

guy." To a pixie, that was a bad thing indeed. "Hellion, just like that chick who killed Willow the other day."

Cruze's head snapped up at that.

"What did he want, then?"

"To kill her, obviously," Hal answered. "Something about a House and some Rite of Decimation. I don't know. The one guy, Craff or Rash or something like that, was talking about it before that Moloch dude showed up."

Cruze nodded. He'd only known Eve for a little while, but he liked her. She was like him. Even their situations were similar. Mostly, though, he liked the living arrangements.

"Eventually, they'll find her," Hal announced, popping open a tiny bottle of booze and taking a swig. "Everyone knows she's hiding in some normal's body. They just have to figure out who it is so they can destroy everything about her."

Cruze didn't like the sound of that.

"Yeah," the cat said, trying to sound only mildly interested. "Well, if I see or hear anything, I'll let you know."

"Really?" asked the pixie. "That'd be fuckin' great. I'll give you ten percent of the finder's fee!"

That caused Cruze to pause. Again, he really liked Eve, but money was money.

"How much is the finder's fee?"

"One hundred bucks."

Cruze sighed. "So you'll give me ten dollars?"

"All right, all right," said the pixie. "I'll make it twenty, but that's as high as I go."

"Right."

CHAPTER 48

*A*ndras was livid to learn that Moloch had failed yet again, but he was glad to hear of the man's death.

"Useless!" he growled as Saffron from House Mathen stood before him, having delivered the grave news. "Did he even have a chance against her?"

"Not really," she replied. "He died pretty quickly, and would have died even sooner had it not been for his protective clothing. On top of that, she'd even promised not to use magic or both her blades."

Andras shook his head and snorted. "Useless."

"Yes, sir," she agreed. "Note that the hellwolf with her is quite formidable as well."

It was aggravating to hear about the power of two people against a mass of highly-trained assassins. Were his own people truly this weak? He couldn't believe that.

"How was it that you survived again?" he challenged.

"I ran from the scene," she replied, "believing that it

was more important to deliver you the information I had learned than to merely lay my life down on principle."

He looked at her eyes as she spoke. They were pointed straight ahead, in military fashion, as she stood there with her hands clasped behind her back.

Saffron was a soldier, plain and simple. She was obviously trained as an assassin as well, but her stature made clear where her base training was focused. That told Andras that her words were true. She knew it was best that her commanding officer be provided detailed information in order to plan next moves.

At the same time, something told Andras that she was the kind of soldier who *took* orders, not one who gave them.

That was actually a benefit, in his perspective.

"You've done well," he said, though it was difficult. "I will be including you again, but will bring along a new team leader."

"Yes, sir," she replied, not flinching in the least.

"That said, you will be on a specific mission that *may* include the killing of Evangeline of House Sinister, but that will *not* be your focus. Your focus will be to monitor the team and report back to me with detailed information so that I may manage them most efficiently." He grunted. "It's clear that my assassins cannot be trusted to handle these missions on their own."

"As you say, sir," she replied.

Andras thought about the best means of handling this going forward. There was still ample time to find and kill the girl, but the sooner she died, the smoother things would go.

Yes, she would definitely need to die soon.

CHAPTER 49

Keep your friends close, and your pets closer.

— GARRICK - HOUSE OF SINISTER

J was sitting in the Grayson residence with my feet up. Cruze was notably absent, which meant he was out on the town again. I'd be lying if I didn't say that made me edgy. The jury was still out on whether or not he was *truly* on my side. Seeing that he was either a demon or a hellion himself, my gut told me he was only on *his* side.

Only time would tell.

Morning would be closing in soon, but I'd told Annette that it had been a hell of a night and that she needed to inform the staff to be quiet until I woke up.

She'd shown me how to close the blackout blinds to keep the room nice and dark. I chose to leave them open for now because I wanted to speak with Cruze…and because the moon was shining through the room beautifully.

Again, I'd chosen the right body to live in.

Fortunately, I hadn't needed to wait for very long before Cruze showed up.

"Where've you been, then?" I asked him as he pushed through the little door by the sex room.

"Out," he replied.

I just stared at him, making it clear that he'd need to use a little more exposition.

He sighed.

"Okay, fine," he said, sitting down in front of me. "Remember that pixie I was telling you about?"

"Hal?" I replied. "I know of him."

"Yeah, well, he apparently got picked up by your boy Moloch. He was roughed up pretty bad, but he'll live."

"Don't care. What did he say?"

"He told Moloch where you were going to be," Cruze continued. "Actually, I'm pretty amazed you're still alive."

I nodded. "You have some interesting friends."

"Says the hellion who is being hunted by some douche named Moloch."

"Not anymore," I replied. "Sent him off on a date with the Vortex."

"Nice."

I shrugged. "Fucker interrupted my dessert."

"Oooh," Cruze said, his face growing serious. "That's a rookie mistake, right there."

I cracked a smile and got up from the chair, heading back toward the bedroom. It was time for a nice, long sleep.

I stopped and looked back at him. He was just watching me walk away.

"You coming?"

His head pulled back. "I thought you didn't want me to sleep in the bed with you."

"Didn't seem to make any difference last night," I pointed out.

"Well, yeah, but...uh..."

"Just stay at my feet this time, got it?"

He dashed past me, jumping onto the bed and moving up to lounge on one of the pillows.

"Got it," he answered, finally.

With a sigh, I climbed in and tried to think happy thoughts.

It'd been a hell of a few days. I missed my old life, even though I hadn't really had a lot of time to dwell on it.

My new life had hit me fast, but so far it wasn't half bad.

Peggy was sweet. A little naive, but that was to be expected. Something told me she would do just about anything to make sure we were safe out in the field. Rainey seemed new, being way too excited about her position in the PPD. She'd grow over time. Annette was still an unknown. She came across as being clever and competent, but until I got to know her better, I couldn't be sure. The Directors were douchey, certainly. My guess was that it just went with the territory.

Q? Him I could have kicked in the nuts multiple times already. I didn't think he was a *bad* guy or anything. I just had the feeling he'd sell his only kid for a day off his sentence.

Kayson was nice, and I had the feeling that something could spring from that relationship. Probably just sexually, but that wasn't such a bad thing...especially when he was wearing a suit.

And then there was Cruze.

I guessed that he was a demon. He was too clever. Hellions could be clever, certainly, but demons were just better at it. That told me that I needed to be even more clever. I'd have to think on precisely how I could manage doing that. People avoided tangling with demons for a reason, after all.

I looked over and found him already fast asleep.

With a smile, I pressed the little button on the wall that slowly closed a massive set of drapes until the room was pitch black.

Yep, this new life wasn't half bad at all.

The End

Thanks for Reading

If you enjoyed this book, would you please leave a review at the site you purchased it from? It doesn't have to be a book report... just a line or two would be fantastic and it would really help us out!

John P. Logsdon
www.JohnPLogsdon.com

John was raised in the MD/VA/DC area. Growing up, John had a steady interest in writing stories, playing music, and tinkering with computers. He spent over 20 years working in the video games industry where he acted as designer and producer on many online games. He's written science fiction, fantasy, humor, and even books on game development. While he enjoys writing lighthearted adventures and wacky comedies most, he can't seem to turn down writing darker fiction.

Christopher P. Young

Chris grew up in the Maryland suburbs. He spent the majority of his childhood reading and writing science fiction and learning the craft of storytelling. He worked as a designer and producer in the video games industry for a number of years as well as working in technology and admin services. He enjoys writing both serious and comedic science fiction and fantasy. Chris lives with his wife and an ever-growing population of critters.

CRIMSON MYTH PRESS

Crimson Myth Press offers more books by this author as well as books from a few other hand-picked authors. From science fiction & fantasy to adventure & mystery, we bring the best stories for adults and kids alike.

www.CrimsonMyth.com